Johnston, Velda
    Shadow Behind the
    rtain

SHADOW
BEHIND
THE
CURTAIN

Also available in Large Print
by Velda Johnston:

The Other Karen
The People from the Sea
A Presence in an Empty Room
The Stone Maiden
Voice in the Night

SHADOW BEHIND THE CURTAIN

Velda Johnston

G.K. HALL & CO.
Boston, Massachusetts
1985

Published in Large Print by arrangement with
Dodd, Mead & Company, Inc.

British Commonwealth rights courtesy of
Blassingame, McCauley and Wood

G.K. Hall Large Print Book Series

Set in 18 pt English Times

Library of Congress Cataloging in Publication Data

Johnston, Velda.
  Shadow behind the curtain.

  (G.K. Hall large print book series)
  1. Large type books. I. Title.
[PS3560.O394S44 1985b]   813'.54   85-8684
ISBN 0-8161-3921-0 (lg. print)

To my niece, SHARON SEYMOUR,
without whose plot contribution
this novel would not have been written.

CHAPTER
ONE

ONCE A PATH must have led to the little house where I had spent the first three years of my life. Now, though, the sparse desert vegetation—small cacti and coarse grass and low bushes of what I thought might be mesquite—covered all the ground between the road and the house.

The front door had no knob, but the shaft was still there. I managed to push the door open. Because it sagged from its upper hinges, its lower edge grated over a floor covered with fine sand.

I stepped into a room that was empty except for a few beer cans, each crushed into a U-shape, in one corner. If the interior walls had ever had any sort of covering—either plaster or paper—it was gone now, leaving horizontal boards with some tarry substance caulking the spaces between them. Someone had blanked off one of the two windows with a rectangle of what looked like plasterboard. Most of the glass was missing from the second window, so that it admitted not only late afternoon sunlight but the faint keening of wind.

Aware of the sound of my footsteps, I crossed the room to the tiny kitchen beyond. The furnishings the kitchen once must have had—a stove, cupboard, and probably a table and chairs—had vanished except for a chipped and stained sink with missing faucets. But this room did show further signs of human habitation, even though I had no way of knowing whether the person who slept here had done so last night or ten years ago. Crumpled in one corner was an old khaki blanket with a battered granite saucepan beside it. Whoever left those objects, I reflected, must have chosen the kitchen as a sleeping place because it was smaller and therefore warmer than the front room. There was only one small window, its glass surprisingly intact, above the sink.

I walked back into the front room and then through a doorway, from which the

2

door was missing, into what must have been my parents' bedroom. Not that any darker areas on the sand-coated floor marked where a bed or bureau had stood. Apparently the furniture had been gone for so long that even its ghostly traces had disappeared.

Next I walked into what unmistakably had been the bathroom, although neither tub, basin, nor toilet remained, only their pipes jutting out from the walls. Beyond the bath was a small room, which I felt must have been mine. Yes, it had to have been. Beside the window a small, irregular patch of wallpaper still clung to the wood. It was a bit of Disney wallpaper, showing the forequarters of a Bambi, legs braced and big eyes curious and friendly as he looked down at a large green frog.

The sight of that bit of faded paper brought an ache to my throat. Poor as they had been, my parents had managed to buy special wallpaper for their infant daughter's room.

Then I realized that through the window I could see into the backyard. Immediately all other thought was overwhelmed by my sense of revulsion. But I had traveled almost three thousand miles to see this house and that backyard, and so I forced myself to walk over to the window.

If there had ever been any sort of outbuilding behind the house, it had vanished. So had the wire fence, which, my mother had told me, my father had put up to protect the peas and onions and carrots they had struggled to grow from this arid New Mexico earth.

And of course the tree was gone, the small cottonwood that, the court had charged, my father had planted in an attempt to hide his crime. And so I had no way of knowing just where it was in this backyard that the body of eight-year-old Daisy McCabe had been buried.

Suddenly I could stay here no longer. Perhaps I would come back later and go over this little house and the barren yard, in the hope, however slim, that after all these years I could find something to prove that my father could never, never have harmed that child or any child. But right now I had to get away from this place.

I walked back through my parents' room and halfway across the living room. Then, a few feet from that sagging front door I stopped, arrested by a memory that had shadowed my otherwise pleasant, even

4

pampered, existence the last twenty-one years of my life.

My father, moving between two men toward that door. The gleam of a narrow metal band one of them had put around his wrist. My mother, her beautiful face white and frozen, her pupils so expanded that her blue eyes looked almost black. And my own small self, paralyzed by a sense that everything that had warmed and sheltered me was dissolving, leaving me to shiver in blasts of icy wind.

Why I never mentioned that memory to my mother until I was twelve years old I don't know. Perhaps it is just that very young children tend to conceal what bothers them most. But a few days short of my thirteenth birthday I walked into her bedroom in the East Seventy-sixth Street Manhattan duplex where I lived with her and my stepfather. She was seated at her dressing table, drawing a comb through silky blond hair that was only a little darker than in my earliest memories of her.

"Mother?"

Her mirrored face, blue-eyed like mine and oval-shaped, but far lovelier than I could hope mine would ever be, smiled at me. She laid down her comb.

"Yes, Deborah?"

"There's something I keep remembering." I paused and then blurted out, "Was my father ever arrested?"

For just an instant something that might have been terror showed in her blue eyes, but it vanished before I could be sure. "Deborah! What on earth makes you ask a question like that?"

I told her about my father being led away between two men.

She laughed and swung around on the dressing table stool to face me. "Darling, you must have seen lots of scenes like that on TV. Or maybe you dreamed it. Anyway, nothing like that ever happened. Joe Hartley was a poor man, but he was never in trouble with the law."

I did not mention that memory to her again. I suppose I wanted to accept my mother's assurance. But I couldn't, not really. And now I was certain that as a very little girl I had stood in this room, perhaps on this very spot, and watched my hand-cuffed father being led out that door.

Movement, glimpsed from the corner of my eye. I whirled to my right.

My heart gave an almost painful thump. A man was looking at me through the shattered glass of one of the windows. A man of forty-odd with coarse black hair, black eyes, and unmistakable Indian features. A new-looking tan leather jacket encased his burly torso.

At the moment his gaze was not hostile, merely curious. Nevertheless, it was with a chill that I realized I was five miles from the nearest town, Prosperity, and at least a mile from the last of the scattered houses I had passed on my way out here.

What was he doing here, on property that once had been a far from flourishing chicken ranch, but was now just a shack surrounded by flat, cactus-spotted desert?

Pulse hammering, I told myself that it was no use trying to run to my rented Datsun, standing out in the road. He could catch me before I reached it. But best not to betray fear. Best to try to disarm him with friendliness, naturalness.

I stretched my lips into a smile. I said, taking a step toward him, "Why, hello!"

To my amazed relief, he turned and ran.

After a moment I walked to the window. A stocky figure in that leather jacket and blue jeans and paratrooper boots, he was still running across the level earth. Then I saw him start to descend into what was apparently a ravine. A second or two later he was no longer visible.

Who was he? Was he the owner of that old blanket and battered saucepan in the kitchen? I didn't think so. Men who bed down in shacks seldom own leather jackets and fairly expensive jeans and boots.

Perhaps he was just some local character who had seen my car parked out front and wondered who was visiting this long-vacant house. But, if so, why had he turned and run when I moved toward him, smiling?

I had no desire to linger here, wondering, in this memory-haunted little house, especially not when it soon would be sunset.

I went outside and with some difficulty closed the door by tugging at the doorknob shaft. Then I hurried to the tan Datsun.

CHAPTER
TWO

ALREADY THE WESTERN sky beyond a line of low hills had turned a pinkish bronze. I started the engine and drove along the two-lane asphalt road, potholed in many places, toward Prosperity.

Even before I had flown out the day before to this extreme southwestern corner of New Mexico, I had learned a lot about the town of Prosperity. My mother had lied to me about my father. But even if she had wanted to, she scarcely could have concealed from me the place of my birth. It was recorded on my birth certificate. And so I kept asking her about the town with the funny name.

A long time ago, she told me, around the turn of the century, Prosperity indeed had been prosperous, thanks to the Gainsworth Silver Mines. But shortly before the First World War the last of the mines had petered out. Even so, the town had continued to flourish in a modest way because of the ranchers from many miles around who shopped there. What was more, the town stood on what was then a busy highway, and thus sold everything from hot dogs to gasoline to souvenirs.

But long before my birth, and even before my mother's, the town's name had become a mockery. The transcontinental superhighway was to blame. Once it was completed, few ranchers continued to shop in Prosperity. Most of them preferred to drive twenty miles or more to the huge shopping complexes that had sprung up near the interstate. As for the travelers who once had filled the town's one hotel and the tourists' cabins on its outskirts, they slept beneath Mr. Howard Johnson's roofs.

I lifted my gaze from the road. On the crest of that line of low hills ahead, silhouetted against the near-sunset sky, I could see what was undoubtedly the Gainsworth house, built by the family whose silver mines had once made Prosperity a flourishing place. My mother had told me that it had been constructed of red sandstone from an Arizona quarry, although now, against that glowing sky, it looked black. Flanked by square crenellated towers, it suggested that it had been built not eighty years ago but a hundred or more, back in the days when its occupants might have had to fire rifles from those towers to repel raiding Indians.

According to what I had heard, a member of the Gainsworth family, Lawrence Gainsworth, still lived there. Fleetingly I wondered why. Surely enough of the family wealth remained that he could have lived elsewhere. And yet he chose to go on living with his daughter in that isolated house above a little town long gone to seed.

Boards rattled under the Datsun's tires as I crossed the bridge over a gully, the same one into which the leather-jacketed man had disappeared. I looked to my right along it for about fifty yards until a curve in the gully walls cut off my view. I could see no sign of him.

Suddenly I wondered if he had known my mother. If so, he might have mistaken me for her. Certainly I looked quite a lot like her, or at least the way she looked when she lived in that little house. Drawn by curiosity, he had peered into that empty room, only to find walking toward him a woman he had not seen for twenty-one years.

Yes, he might have mistaken me for her. But even so, why had he fled? It was hard to think of anyone being afraid of my gentle mother.

And that, of course, brought me to another thought. With a mixture of revulsion and hope, I wondered if I could have seen beyond that shattered windowpane the man who in actuality had committed that crime, the terrible crime for which my young father had been tried and sentenced.

Perhaps I should go to Prosperity's chief of police immediately and try to learn the identity of the man with the coarse black hair and Indian features. But already I'd had one interview with the chief or rather, acting chief, since, as he had curtly informed me, he was standing in for his temporarily disabled father, the duly elected chief. My conversation with him had been so unpleasant, though, that I still smarted from it. Better wait until tomorrow, when I might have a better chance of keeping my temper. After all, I might need Acting Chief Benjamin Farrel's cooperation if my trip out here was to be anything except a waste of time and money.

The road had widened to become the town's main street. Although sunset still glowed in the sky, lights had been turned on in a few buildings. I passed the drugstore, the Bluebell Luncheonette, a small furniture store. The marquee of the Gem Theater was lighted, advertising the sort of Grade Z cowboy movie that is exhibited only in tiny towns in the Middle and Far West.

Next to the theater was the red brick Town Hall, one half of which housed the police station. The lights were on in the station's outer office. Through the plate-glass window I saw Ben Farrel standing tall and sandy-haired beside an overweight, dark-haired young man who sat at a desk, hunched over a typewriter. Evidently Farrel was chewing his subordinate out about something, because his bony face looked as harsh as it had the day before, when he told me I was wasting my time and his.

Suddenly I wondered if he was married. If so, I felt sorry for his wife.

And that thought, inevitably, brought me to a realization I kept trying to keep at bay, a realization of the possible wreckage of my own marriage prospects. No, not possible;

almost certain. In the past month my whole comfortable world had collapsed. How could I expect what I'd had with Greg not to be a part of the destruction?

I flicked on my headlights, drove another two blocks, and then turned into the parking lot beside the Hotchkiss Hotel. In the second or two before I turned my lights off I saw painted, in faded letters on the building's red brick wall, an advertisement that might have been as old as the hotel itself: GERSON'S LIVERY STABLE, HORSES BY THE DAY, WEEK, OR MONTH.

I locked the car and went around to the hotel entrance.

CHAPTER
THREE

THE SMALL LOBBY was empty except for the desk clerk, a thin, youngish man with a slight stammer, and a bald man who sat in one of the sagging leather chairs, his face partially hidden behind an outspread copy of the *Luna Press*. I asked for my key. Rather than ride up in the palsied elevator, I climbed a flight of stairs to my second-floor room.

In a way, that room was even more depressing than the empty little house five miles east of town. The bed of cheap blond wood, bought perhaps thirty years before, was covered by a thin, damask patterned spread of a peculiarly awful shade of pink. The dark brown draperies, although not visibly stained, certainly needed cleaning.

They exuded the smell of countless cigars and cigarettes that had been smoked in this room. Some of them had burned worm-shaped scars on the bureau and the small bedside table that held a lamp with an amber glass base and fake parchment shade. The tan wallpaper bore a design that I would not have believed if I hadn't seen it. Jagged black lines, which looked like nothing so much as strands of barbed wire, spaced about six inches apart, ran from the baseboards to the ceiling. No pictures of any sort adorned the walls, although squares and rectangles of less faded paper marked where pictures once had hung.

Again, as when I arrived here the previous day, I thought of asking the clerk to show me another room. But no. While I was registering he had told me with pride that he would give me the best room in the house, "a big corner room with two windows, and as far from the elevator as you can get." Besides, I might as well get used to grimness. After all, it appeared that my foreseeable future was to be bleak indeed.

It was as if Fortune, which had indulged me extravagantly for all except the first few of my twenty-four years, had suddenly decided to redress the balance. And so it was that I found myself, not in the luxurious apartment that had been home to me for nearly all my life, but in this ugly New Mexico hotel room.

I have only the most fragmentary memories of the West Side apartment that my mother and I occupied for the first few months after, on borrowed money, she had brought me to Manhattan. I know it was a sixth-floor walk-up, with steps so steep that my not yet four-year-old legs had to stretch to the utmost to climb them. The apartment must have been inexpensive indeed. Working as a waitress, the only sort of gainful employment for which she could claim experience, my mother couldn't have been able to afford much rent, especially after paying the woman two blocks away who baby-sat in her own apartment for several working mothers.

We didn't stay in that apartment long. My mother had been working at one of a chain of restaurants for only a few weeks when the owner of the chain came in one day on an inspection tour. He must have made it his immediate business to learn her name and phone number, because the next day he called and asked her to go to dinner with him.

Years later, when my mother finally considered me old enough to receive such confidences, she told me about her anxiety over that first date with Lou Channing. "I was almost sure that he would want me to go to his apartment, and that when I refused he would have me fired."

Instead, after a meal in one of New York's finest restaurants, he accompanied my mother in a taxi to the babysitter's and then carried me, sleeping, up five flights of stairs, handed me into her arms, unlocked the door for her, and said good night.

Until their fourth date, he didn't even try to kiss her. And on their fifth date, he asked her to marry him.

"Lou liked the idea that I'd always been poor," she once told me. "He said what would be the kick in buying me furs and jewelry if I'd been used to such things.

"Besides," she added, "It wasn't as if he himself had been born rich. He started out as a busboy. It wasn't until he got to be a waiter at Henri Soule's restaurant that he made good tips, and saved his money, and started investing in the stock market—"

For about a year after their marriage we lived in a smallish apartment on Fifth Avenue. Then he bought the duplex on East

18

Seventy-sixth Street, two entire floors with a total of twelve rooms.

A Cinderella story? No, not quite. Cinderella's prince was young and handsome. Lou, twenty-odd years older than my mother, was a widower with two grown sons. What was more, he loved food—which was probably why he invested his stock market gains in the restaurant business—and so tended to be a little pudgy despite strenuous bouts of dieting.

But I am sure that my mother was happy with him, just as I am sure she loved him, although with an affection that must have been partly that of a daughter. I also loved him. I had every reason to. He not only adopted me legally, thus changing my last name from Hartley to Channing. He fussed over me as if I were indeed his child, born to him in his middle age. He joined my mother in careful studies of catalogs, not only of private schools but of summer camps. He kept track of my grades. Several times he took me to the dentist when my mother was otherwise occupied. He made sure that my tennis and riding and ballet instructors were the best available.

In answer to my persistent questions during those years of my growing up, my mother told me in bits and pieces about her own early years. To me it sounded almost as exotic as a childhood spent in an Amazon jungle. She had no memory whatever of her parents, a young Illinois couple named Campbell. Bringing their infant daughter Sara with them they had come to join the wife's great-aunt at a religious colony west of the little town of Prosperity, New Mexico. Admission to the sect, they found, was not a simple matter. Before accepting new members, the colony's elders spent days in prayerful deliberations. While they waited to learn their fate, the Campbells and their four-month-old baby lived in their camper, parked beside a small stream running through an arroyo a few miles from the colony itself.

Spring rains were torrential that year. One night a dam in the hills west of the area crumbled, and a wall of muddy water swept down the narrow canyon. When day broke, searchers found the wreckage of the camper strewn along the arroyo's sloping sides, but the bodies of the young couple, swept a mile downstream, weren't found until two days later.

It was illness that had saved the life of the infant who grew up to be my mother.

Because she had a feverish cold, the Campbells, three days before the dam's bursting, had sought and obtained permission to place small Sara in the colony's infirmary.

Since the Campbells had no close relatives either willing or able to take the baby in, the county authorities decreed that in effect she would be adopted by the colony, although the adoption papers named only Sara's great-aunt. Even though the old lady lived until Sara was six, the child was cared for from the first by the whole community.

"I did not mind," my mother told me. "All the children there were raised like that. The colony disapproved of close family ties. Every adult was supposed to feel equal concern for all the children, no matter whom they'd been born to."

By the time my mother reached her late teens, the colony was in financial straits, mostly because of a plunge in the sales of its handmade quilts and furniture. At last the elders decided that for the sake of the colony as a whole, they would have to do something they had never done before—send a few of their younger members out into the sinful world to earn money for the sect.

Two of the young men went to work as fence riders on a cattle ranch near the Mexican border. The colony kept Sara, whose beauty must have seemed downright alarming to the puritans who had raised her, much closer to home. One of the elders arranged for her to work as counter girl at the Peerless Diner in Prosperity.

Her first afternoon there, a young man came in for a cup of coffee. His name was Joe Hartley, and he was trying to make a living out of a run-down chicken ranch he had inherited from an uncle. He came back the next day, and the next, and the next. Before two weeks had passed, he and Sara drove in his truck to Las Cruces and got married.

Although my mother at times could be quite voluble about her childhood and young girlhood, she always seemed reluctant indeed to talk about the four years she had lived with my father. But the summer after I completed my junior year at Radcliffe, I came back to Manhattan determined to learn more about those four years. After all, they included the first years of my own life, and so surely I had a right to know at least a little more than I did.

One June night she and I sat in white

22

wrought-iron chairs in the garden behind the East Seventy-sixth Street duplex. The unceasing sound of traffic was only a murmur back there, scarcely louder than the splashing of the fountain in the small marble fish pond a few feet away. The warm darkness was unbroken except for the light from rear windows in a lofty apartment house on Seventy-seventh Street.

I said, "I've been thinking about that religious colony in New Mexico. They must have been very upset when you ran away and got married."

She and Lou and I had drunk a quart of champagne at dinner to celebrate my homecoming from college. Perhaps that was why she was more communicative than usual about that period of her life. "Yes, they were outraged. Nathaniel Crisp, especially. But I was nineteen. There was nothing they could do about it."

"Who was Nathaniel Crisp?" She had never mentioned him before.

"Oh, a young man at the colony. He'd asked the elders for permission to marry me. I didn't know that, and even if I had it would have made no difference. I would have refused him. But anyway, he came to the house one afternoon when Joe wasn't there and started thundering at me like an Old Testament prophet. All about how a marriage unsanctioned by the elders was the same as fornication. I managed to get rid of him before your father came home."

"Mother, were you and my father happy together?"

"Oh, yes. So very happy." She added quickly, "I mean we were for the first few months."

Another lie, at least an implicit one. They must have been happy for more than a few months, because I was certain that I had been a part of that happiness. It was nothing as concrete as a memory. Rather it was just an impression of my very small self sitting in something—a stroller, perhaps? —with sunlight warm on my face and hands. My mother and father were sitting near me, perhaps on the front or back steps of their house. She was doing something with her hands, something that made a ping, ping sound. Probably she was shelling peas into a colander. As they talked, she was smiling at him. I could not understand their words, of course. But I could hear the lilt in their voices. And I had what I recognized later on as a sense of infinite safety and serenity, wrapping the three of us like a warm blanket.

I said, "And yet you divorced him."

I don't know when I first learned that my parents were divorced. I just know that by the time my mother brought me to New York I realized that they were, even though I had only the vaguest notion of what the word *divorce* meant.

My mother, sitting opposite me in the darkened city garden, made no reply.

I persisted, "Why did you divorce him?"

"After a while we found we just—couldn't get along. I suppose it was my fault, mostly. I hated that chicken ranch, hated never having enough money for even ordinary things, like new window curtains. The ranch had never been much of a success. Our third year together he'd had to take out a mortgage on the place, as well as start doing odd jobs all over town, just to keep our heads above water. Finally we decided to sell the place, split the few hundred that would be left after we paid off the mortgage, and go our separate ways."

I knew that could not be the whole explanation. My mother never would have let lack of money separate her from a man she loved. In fact, I was sure that if my stepfather lost everything he owned, including this luxurious duplex, she would not only stick with him but, if necessary, get a job.

"And you have no idea where my father is now?"

"I don't. I've told you so every time you asked that question."

Sharpness in her voice now, but I sensed that it sprang less from annoyance than from some kind of fear.

Nevertheless, I persisted for a moment more. "Maybe he went to some relatives."

"Deborah, I've told you time and again. By the time your father grew up he didn't have any relatives. No one except the uncle who left him the ranch, and he'd been an old bachelor."

Could that be true? Surely almost everyone had some sort of relative. Perhaps she was afraid that if I knew my father had relatives in Nebraska, say, I might try to get in touch with them—

"Deborah, please!" The light from the apartment house windows showed me the beseeching look on my mother's face. "Must we talk about—unhappy times? Wouldn't you rather talk about moving down to the beach cottage?"

The "cottage" was a French Provincial

house of six bedrooms on East Hampton's Georgica Pond. Lou had bought it two years earlier.

"Of course," I said. "When are we going there?"

After that I gave up trying to gain information she was so unwilling to give me. And I tried not to let my ignorance bother me as I moved through my final year at Radcliffe and then into a Wall Street brokerage firm, where I hoped that in time I would become a security analyst. Why should I let my lack of knowledge of my earliest years shadow my highly enjoyable present?

And then, when I had been out of college two years, my life became more than enjoyable. It became wonderful. One August afternoon, as I sat on the terrace of East Hampton's Old Colony Club, I met Gregory Vanlieden.

Lou and my mother and I were not members of the club. It does not take kindly to ex-busboys, even ones who have grown rich enough to own Manhattan duplexes and Georgica Pond summer houses. But frequently I was the guest of friends who were members. I was sitting with two such friends, a newly married couple named

Binnie and Charlie Marsden, when Greg came walking along the terrace and stopped at our table. Binnie made the introductions and asked him to join us.

Until then I hadn't realized just how handsome a man could be. Oddly enough, considering that he was the descendant of a long line of American patricians dating from Dutch colonial times, Greg had an Italian look—waving dark hair, gray eyes, a beautifully cut mouth with a sensually full lower lip. And even in a casual white shirt and white duck trousers, he had an air of easy elegance.

From the first moment I felt overwhelmingly attracted to him. And I knew, as a woman does know those things, that he felt drawn to me. That alarmed me. I must not let him think that I was "old rich," as he and the Marsdens were. Better to let him know as soon as possible, rather than later on, when I might find his rejection of me nothing less than shattering.

My opportunity came a few minutes later. Binnie referred to herself as a "Turk." Her father had been the American ambassador to Turkey at the time of her birth.

I said, keeping my tone light, "My birthplace was pretty exotic, too. I was born on a highly unsuccessful chicken ranch in New Mexico.''

Binnie, a classmate of mine at Radcliffe, was a smart girl. From the wryly sympathetic glance she threw me I know that she realized just why I had hurried to tell Greg Vanlieden of my origins. She said, ''What was the funny name of that town near the chicken ranch?''

''Prosperity.''

I had been looking at Greg when I mentioned the chicken ranch and had seen his startled expression. But now, when I looked back at him, he was smiling. ''A New Mexico chicken ranch! I'll have to hear about that.''

A few minutes later he suggested that the four of us stay at the club for dinner. And before he dropped me off at the Georgica Pond house that night we made a dinner date for the next evening, this time for just the two of us.

We dated all the rest of the summer and early fall, in the Hamptons on weekends and once or even twice in the city during the week. Like me, Greg worked on Wall Street. He was an account executive in a brokerage house. It seemed to me that our

29

having similar careers made our relationship almost unbelievably perfect. I fell deeper and deeper in love. Sometimes just the sight of his hand on the steering wheel, the slender but strong brown wrist encircled by a gold watchband and above that the snowy white cuff, could make me feel weak.

I told him more about my origins. I told him of my mother's growing up in that religious colony, and of my father's failure to made a decent living—a failure that, according to my mother, was responsible for their divorce. If my talk of a background so different from his own disturbed Greg, he did not show it.

Several times that fall and early winter Greg took me to his family house up the Hudson, one of the few Hudson River mansions still occupied by descendants of the original builders. His parents, both tall, both with traces of the good looks that so overwhelmed me in their son, treated me with warm friendliness. If they were a mite dismayed to find Greg smitten with a girl whose father had been a failed chicken rancher, and whose stepfather was a self-made man who started out as a busboy, they did not betray it. I gained an impression that this aging couple would not want to oppose their youngest child and only son in any choice he might make. When they invited me to spend Christmas Eve with them, I was sure that Greg intended to ask me to marry him, and that they knew it.

Less than two weeks after Christmas my stepfather, still fighting his battle against overweight, dropped dead during a squash game in a lower Manhattan athletic club.

For me, his sudden death was not the blow it was for my mother. Nevertheless, I grieved for him, that modest, warm-hearted man who had taken my mother and me from a sixth-floor walk-up and given us every comfort and luxury it was in his power to give.

One night, about three weeks after Lou's death, Greg and I started driving up to his parents' house. About halfway there, he stopped in a turnoff above the black river and asked me to marry him.

Held close in his arms, my cheek against his warm dark cheek, I gave him his answer. He said, "Shall we tell your mother now, or shall we wait until she's had more time to recover from your stepfather's death?"

We decided to wait a couple of weeks.

But when I finally told my mother, over the fireside table in the library where we'd dined ever since Lou's death, her response was so joyous that I wished I had let her know earlier. The tears streaming down her face told me how much she had feared that my love for a man of a background so different from mine would lead me to heartbreak.

We discussed plans for a June wedding at St. Thomas's. "And would you and Greg like to have the reception at the Plaza?"

I said, in surprise, "Not here?"

"Deborah, there's something I've been keeping from you. I'm going to have to sell the duplex. I didn't want to tell you right away, not when I could see how tense you were, waiting for Greg to propose. But anyway, our lawyer tells me that for the past three years Lou's restaurants have been losing a great deal of money."

"But he never said anything about it. He never asked us to economize."

"I suppose he kept thinking that matters would right themselves. In the meantime, he didn't want to deny us anything—"

She gave a shaky laugh. "Deborah! Don't look like that. I'm not going to have to go back to waiting tables. But I do need to sell this huge place and find a small apartment. A small one is all I'll need, now that you're getting married.''

She frowned. ''Moving isn't going to be easy. All this furniture, all these things to be gotten rid of one way or another—''

''I'll help. Tomorrow is Saturday. I can spend the whole day making lists of what you want to keep and what you want to sell.''

Secure in my happiness, I spoke so lightly. I was like some carefree motorist, unaware that at the next intersection he will crash head-on into a truck.

Now, standing at the window of this frowzy hotel room, I looked down into the wide main street, empty except for a pickup truck rattling past, and thought of that Saturday nearly a month before, that day when I learned what had happened twenty-one years ago in this, the town of my birth.

CHAPTER
FOUR

I BEGAN THAT Saturday morning by con-
ferring with Mrs. Reid, our plump,
pleasant-faced housekeeper for the past ten
years, in her sitting room on the flat's lower
floor.

She said, "It might be easiest to start
with the rooms Charlie Won and Julia used
to have, since there's nothing in those two
rooms except basic furniture."

Julia was the lady's maid Lou had insisted that my mother hire. Charlie Won, a
Taiwanese, had barbered my stepfather and
kept his personal belongings in order for
about a dozen years. Since Lou's death,
both Julia and Won had left us for other
employers. My mother had given me the
impression that their leaving had been their

own idea. But now I realized that probably she herself, in the interests of economy, had found other places for them.

We went into Won's room first. Mrs. Reid gave an annoyed exclamation. "I'd forgotten about his books. He said he'd drop by and pick them up, but he hasn't. Well, I'll just have to get in touch with him at his new place." Beside the single bed, stripped now of everything except its rolled-up mattress, was a small bookcase of some sort of fiberboard, crammed with books. I'd always known that Won, although a man of little formal education, had a thirst for learning. Each fall he had signed up for night courses at the New School for Social Research. Now, curious to see just what his interests had been, I walked over to the bookcase. "Maybe you'd better start in Julia's room," I said to Mrs. Reid over my shoulder. "I'll join you soon."

"All right. If you don't find me there I'll be in the butler's pantry. There's all that china and silverware to list." She left the room.

Almost instantly I realized that Won was a legal buff. Except for a few volumes of history, his books pertained to law. There was a Blackstone, and bound copies of the

35

Yale Law Review, and Clarence Darrow's autobiography, and a number of similar volumes, including a paperback edition of a book entitled *My Ten Most Memorable Cases*.

I suppose I drew that book out from among the others because I had once tuned in on a Dick Cavett interview with its author. Anyway, I turned to the Table of Contents and scanned the chapter titles: "The Dog that *Did* Bark in the Night"; "The Lady Widowed Once Too Often"; "Ill Fortune in a Town Called Prosperity."

I stood motionless, staring down at the page. How many towns in the United States were named Prosperity? A half dozen? Three? One?

On legs that felt weighted, I crossed to the room's only armchair, sat down, and began to read the book's third chapter:

To me, the case involving the murder of little Daisy McCabe will always seem one of my most baffling. Oh, not that there was any question of Joseph Hartley's guilt. The evidence against him was overwhelming. True, it was all circumstantial, but it almost always is in cases of that sort. Not many people kidnap and murder a child in front of witnesses.

No, what still puzzles me about the case is how a man like Joseph Hartley, a young man liked and respected by almost everyone in his small community, could have committed such an atrocious act.

The print seemed to blur momentarily. Joseph Hartley, my father.

Beneath my shock there was an even more hideous sense of familiarity, as if long years ago, at a time lost to my conscious memory, I had known at least a part of what I was about to read.

After a few moments my vision cleared, and I was able to go on to the next paragraph.

Daisy McCabe, eight years old, lived in a little New Mexico town called Prosperity, a once flourishing community fallen upon such lean days that its name had an ironic ring. A few months after I was appointed district attorney for two counties in the southwestern part of the state, Daisy disappeared.

Apparently she had been a neglected child all her short life. Deserted by her father, she lived with her mother, Loretta McCabe, and Loretta's common-law husband. Daisy was a frequent truant from school. Often she was seen wandering along the roads, trying to hitch rides and sometimes succeeding.

It was this habit of hers which, after her disappearance, first drew attention to Joseph Hartley. A woman reported that she had seen Daisy riding in the old truck he used for transporting chickens to and from his eight-acre chicken ranch. What was more, Loretta McCabe said that lately her child had been prattling about someone named Joe. Loretta, paying little attention to her child's talk, had not even asked her for Joe's last name.

Then someone remembered that Joe Hartley recently had planted a cottonwood sapling in the backyard of the little house he occupied with his wife and daughter, a child of three. Armed with a search warrant, Prosperity's Police Chief Benjamin Farrel went out to the Hartley place and uprooted the tree. Three feet below where the roots had rested they had found Daisy's fully clothed body, with bruises still visible on her throat. (She had died of strangulation, the autopsy later determined.) In her still-clenched right hand there was an irregularly shaped object, about the size of a marble. It was a nugget of iron pyrite, or fool's gold, of the sort men used to wear many years ago on their watch chains. Joe admitted that the nugget was his. It had been among the effects of the uncle from whom he had inherited his ranch. Hartley said he had carried it as a kind of "lucky pocket piece," but had lost it somewhere about a week before Daisy's disappearance.

In spite of the overwhelming evidence against him, Hartley never ceased to protest his innocence. The court-appointed defense attorney tried to persuade him to plead insanity, but he adamantly refused.

With evidence like that, I had no trouble in obtaining a conviction. The judge sentenced him to the state prison near Las Cruces for the rest of his natural life. As of this writing he is still there.

But after all these years the case still haunts me. For one thing, Daisy McCabe had not been sexually molested. In every other case in my experience, a kidnapped child has been murdered for one of two reasons. Either the killer was a pervert who wanted to keep his small victim from identifying him, or he was a kidnapper for profit who panicked at the thought that, even if the ransom was paid, the child's testimony might bring about his arrest. Daisy had not died at the hands of a sexual pervert. And not even a man of the dimmest intelligence could have hoped to obtain ransom money from Loretta McCabe or her common-law husband, both of whom had been "on the county" most of their lives.

Another thing was that Hartley had so much to live for, so much to stay out of prison for. True, his chicken ranch brought him only a bare subsistence. Not even that, because he had to supplement his income by doing odd jobs—carpentry and plumbing and so on—all over town. But his blond young wife was one of the most beautiful women I have ever seen. Furthermore, the way she kept her gaze fixed upon him at the trial, obviously waiting for him to look at her so that she could send him a smile of love and encouragement, left no doubt of her devotion. And although I never saw his little girl—she was never present in the courtroom— I knew from my first interview with him in my office that he was tormented by the thought that because of him his little girl's life might be ruined.

Yes, Joseph Hartley killed Daisy McCabe. I'm convinced of it, the jury was convinced, and so was the judge. The only question is: why did Hartley do it?

CHAPTER
FIVE

I DON'T REMEMBER walking from Won's room to the butler's pantry. I do remember Mrs. Reid standing in front of a shelf of cut-glass water tumblers, pencil poised above the notebook in her hand. I said, "I don't feel well. I'm going upstairs."

Her gaze, both concerned and curious, went from my face to the paperback book I carried, forefinger marking the place. "Can I get you anything?"

"No, thank you."

On the flat's upper floor I found my mother seated at the desk in what had been Lou's study. Chin resting on her elbow-propped hand, she was frowning down at what appeared to be a small stack of bills.

"Mother."

She turned to me. "Oh, good! Maybe you can explain this bill from the heating oil people." Then her face lost color. "Deborah! What is it?"

Perhaps I could have approached the matter more gently, but I was still too stunned to even think of doing so. I handed her the opened book. I think that even before she looked down at it she somehow guessed what the book had told me, because her face turned a shade whiter.

I walked over to the window and looked down into the winter-bleak garden, its rose trellis bare, its fish pond empty, its flagstone path strewn with dead leaves. I heard my mother give a low moan. Then for several minutes there was silence except for the rustle of turning pages.

She called my name. I turned around. Utter despair in the blue eyes. It was then that I felt, despite my shock, and my resentment at having been kept in ignorance, and my terror of what my newfound knowledge would do to Greg and me—despite all that, I felt a rush of concern for her.

She said brokenly, "Oh, my baby! You can't know how many nights I've prayed that you would never find out."

"So it's true." Until then, when it died, I

hadn't realized that I had held the absurd hope that somehow it was not.

"Yes. No. I mean, all that about his arrest and conviction is true. But your father did not kill that child. I know he did not."

I might have asked her how she knew, but I didn't, because I was sure her answer would be, "I just know, that's all."

"Is my father still alive?"

"Yes, and still—still—"

"In prison? Are you in touch with him at all?"

"Of course I am!" A defensive note in the distraught voice now. "I write to him, and he writes to me. He sends the letters in care of Barry Greenwood." Greenwood had been our family lawyer for the past fifteen years. "I—I couldn't have them come here."

"Because of me? Or because of Lou, too? I mean, did he know—"

"Of course he knew! Do you think I would have married him without telling him about Joe? And the divorce," she rushed on, "I didn't want it, but Joe insisted. He said that for both your sake and mine, it had to be.

"It was Lawrence Gainsworth who paid

44

for it," she added. "Remember my telling you about him, the rich man who lived up in the hills near Prosperity? He loaned me enough to pay for a divorce lawyer, and your expenses and mine in Reno, and our plane tickets to New York."

After a moment I said, "Did you know about this book?" I looked to where it lay face downward beside the stack of bills.

She shook her head. "You know I don't read much."

She didn't. Fashion magazines and an occasional light romance. That was about it.

I said dully, "Dick Cavett interviewed that district attorney quite a while ago."

"I didn't know."

It wasn't likely that she would have. She watched Channel Thirteen only when they were showing old movies.

She said, "But I do know that that district attorney died about a year ago. I suppose it was in the papers, but I didn't see it. It was Joe who told me about it in one of his letters."

I too had read no newspaper account of the district attorney's death.

"Deborah, what about Greg?"

"I'll tell him. He has to know about my father."

Her eyes looked enormous in her white face. "When will you tell him?"

"Tonight. There's no point in putting it off."

Her face crumpled. "Oh, my darling. Your father and I, we so hoped that you would never be harmed by what had happened to him. We wanted you to grow up happy, and have a wonderful marriage. And when I saw that you were falling in love with Greg, I felt such joy for you, and yet so much fear—"

I said heavily, "I realize you must have."

"How do you think Greg—"

"How will he take it? We'll see."

Greg and I had planned to have dinner that night at a new Japanese restaurant on East Fifty-fifth Street. But at three o'clock I phoned him and suggested that, as we had several times before, we cook dinner together in his apartment near Lincoln Center.

"Great. You know I always enjoy that."

I had enjoyed it, too. Our table set up before the fireplace, show tunes or perhaps

46

Vivaldi or Brahms on the stereo and, after the meal, sitting on cushions on the floor with our coffee cups and perhaps some brandy.

He went on, "If you're still in a Japanese mood, how about beef teriyaki in the wok? I'll go down right now and pick out the steak."

I said, with an effort, "That will be fine."

"Debby, is something wrong?"

"Yes. But I don't want to talk about it over the phone. I'll tell you when I see you."

We never had that wok dinner. Unable to bear my anxiety any longer, I handed him the book almost as soon as I entered his apartment.

"What's this?"

"It's about my father. Just open it at the bookmark and start reading."

Puzzlement in the handsome face beneath the dark, loosely waving hair. "This is about Lou Channing?"

"No, my real father, the man my mother divorced. Oh, Greg! Please just read it."

He sat down in one corner of the sofa. I sat down in the other corner and fixed my gaze on my clasped hands. I heard his sharp intake of breath, and then nothing at all for a while except the sound of turning pages. Finally I heard not even that. I raised my gaze.

He was looking at me, his face so white that I was reminded, fleetingly, of a marble Apollo. "Is this some kind of, kind of—"

"Hoax? No, it all happened like that, except that my mother says he wasn't guilty. But then of course she would say that. She loved him. She probably still does."

"Then he's still alive?"

"Yes."

The gray eyes looked even more appalled. I could tell what he was thinking. Joe Hartley, alive, and perhaps to be released some day, despite that life sentence. Joe Hartley, convicted child murderer, and his future father-in-law.

"When did you—when did you—"

"I learned about it just today, when I found this book. It was in Won's old room." I felt a hysterical impulse to laugh. "You remember Charlie Won, who looked after Lou."

Greg did not answer. I could understand the resentment, the near bitterness in his eyes. Out of his love for me, he had disregarded the fact of my background, so different from his own. But he had been kept in the dark about the most important thing concerning me. And so now he, Gregory Vanlieden, found himself pledged to marry the daughter of a man imprisoned for the sort of crime that even other convicts considered heinous.

I said, "Oh, Greg! Please! Don't look at me like that. Don't! I can't bear it!"

I began to cry, hands covering my face. Immediately he came over and sat beside me and took me in his arms. "Oh, darling! None of it is your fault. You didn't know. And I love you so much, Debby, so very much."

He broke off and then added, in an almost desperate voice, "It's just that my parents are very apt to find out, one way or another, even if we decided to try to keep it from them. And as you know, my mother's heart isn't strong."

I said wretchedly, my cheek against his shoulder, "You don't want to marry me now, do you?"

His arms tightened around me. "I do want to! You can't know how much." After a moment he went on, his voice dull now, "But families have to be considered, too. At least we Vanliedens have always felt families had to be.''

I tried to steady my voice. ''What are you saying? That we should both—think about it?''

After a moment he said, ''Yes, I guess that's what I mean.''

''Suppose we don't see each other for three weeks.''

Perhaps half a minute passed before he answered. ''I guess that would be best. Three weeks should be time enough for us to think things through.''

I sat up then and pressed the heels of my palms against my eyes for a few seconds, willing my tears to stop. ''I'll go now,'' I said. ''I don't think either of us feels like dinner.''

He helped me on with my coat. For a while we stood embraced, my arms locked around his neck, his lips pressing mine. Then I picked up the book he had placed on the sofa's end table and walked out of his apartment.

CHAPTER
SIX

THERE IS AN old saying that disasters seldom come singly. Perhaps that is true. But when one disaster closely follows another, I don't think it is just a matter of happenstance. I believe one disaster flows from another.

I'm sure that it was true in my mother's case. It wasn't just by chance that, less than two weeks after my last meeting with Greg, my mother tried to cross Madison Avenue in midblock through heavy afternoon traffic. I think she was so preoccupied with her misery and guilt that she didn't realize what she was doing.

When I came home that Saturday night after my last visit to Greg's apartment, I had told her that we had decided not to see each other for three weeks. "Oh, darling!"

she had cried. "Don't you think that's foolish? Was this three week's parting his idea?"

"I was the one who suggested it."

"Oh, my baby! Then you are foolish. You shouldn't give him a chance to feel that perhaps he can get along without you."

"If there's a chance he'll feel that, then I don't want him. Nothing could be more humiliating than marrying a man who's reluctant to marry you. And now let's don't talk about it. Please, Mother."

She did not talk about it again. But I could tell that Greg and I were seldom out of her thoughts. I could almost hear her thinking that perhaps she should have remained married to my father and stayed in Prosperity, where any man attracted to me would know from the first that my father was serving a life sentence. Perhaps she should never have brought me to New York, and certainly never have married Lou Channing, thus making it possible for me to meet the very sort of man who would be most unwilling to bring a convict's daughter into his family.

For a week and a half, while I went to the office each weekday and at night helped her list the duplex's furnishings, I could tell

52

that, just as I was, she was hoping for Greg to call me. He did not. Preoccupied as I was with my own misery, I still was aware that she seemed to grow a little thinner and paler each day.

At my office, around three o'clock on a Wednesday afternoon, I received a call from Lenox Hill Hospital. My mother had been struck down by a taxi, and was now in the emergency ward.

She died before I got there.

During the days that followed I had that sense of frozen isolation that marks the first stage of grief. But in actual fact I was far from alone. I had Mrs. Reid's presence, familiar and comforting but never intrusive. As the news spread, more and more friends called, asking if there was anything, "anything at all," that they could do. Barry Greenwood, our family lawyer, visited me frequently.

And Greg was with me. He arrived at the duplex less than an hour after I came home from the hospital and held me closely, silently, in his arms. In my distraught state I didn't even think to ask him how he had heard the news, but I imagine it was our mutual friend Binnie Marsden who had called him.

Four nights after the funeral—St. Thomas's Episcopal had been filled to capacity, and I discovered then that there was comfort in having so many join in the final farewell—a night with prematurely springlike warmth in the air, Greg and I walked from the duplex to the park overlooking the East River. For a while, not speaking, we leaned against an iron handrail, eyes fixed on the black, faintly luminous river moving endlessly toward the sea. Then Greg said, "How soon do you think we should marry?"

For days I had known he was going to say something like that, and so I had my answer ready. "Greg, you mustn't feel we should marry just because my mother—I mean, such a marriage wouldn't be good enough for either of us."

"It's not just because of that! I love you."

"I know you do. But I also know that you hate the thought of marrying Joseph Hartley's daughter. You would find it unbearable to tell your parents about him, and equally unbearable to marry me without telling them. You couldn't stand the constant dread that they would find out."

He did not deny it. In the light of a

nearby standard lamp his face was wretched. "Then what should we do?"

"Wait. Wait until I get back from New Mexico."

"New Mexico!"

"I'm going back to that little town where it all happened. I'm going to see if I can discover anything, anything at all, that might help him get released. And I'm going to that prison, of course."

After a while Greg said in a dull voice, "I don't suppose there'd be any use in my trying to persuade you that we both should just accept the idea of his guilt, and then try to handle matters as best we can."

"No use at all. Now that I know the truth, I couldn't live with my conscience if I didn't go to him and do all I can for him. And there's you and me. As I see it, our only chance of happiness together lies in finding out that my father didn't do that —that terrible thing."

I added abruptly, "Let's go back now. I'm cold."

After a moment he said, "All right. But as soon as you get to that little town, will you let me know where you're staying?"

"Of course."

In silence we walked back to my place. At

the door I didn't ask him in for a drink, nor did he suggest it. He unlocked the door for me. He kissed me and held me close, his cheek warm against mine. Then he walked down the block to where he'd parked his BMW.

At ten the next morning Barry Greenwood phoned me at my office. Would I please come to his office at my earliest convenience? He had matters to discuss with me concerning my mother's estate. I had intended to ask him for an appointment, and so I agreed to be there at five-thirty.

I found Greenwood in his luxurious private office in the otherwise deserted suite. Light from his desk lamp, shaded in green leather, shone on the broad face, shrewd and yet kindly, of the lawyer I had known for most of my life.

"I hate to bother you with legal and financial matters at a time like this, Deborah, but I need your signature on a few documents."

"Of course."

"Your mother's will isn't ready for probate yet, but as I'm sure you know, she has made a bequest of twenty thousand to Mrs. Reid and left everything else to you."

I nodded.

"The trouble is that everything else won't amount to much."

"I know. Mother told me that Lou had been losing money for several years. She said the duplex would have to be sold."

"The duplex, and the East Hampton house, too. The situation is worse than your mother realized. Lou heavily mortgaged both properties over a year ago, so their sale won't bring you much." He added quickly, "Oh, I'm not saying you'll have to sell matches on street corners, but you're going to be a long, long way from rich."

"I don't think I'll mind too much." I meant it. Compared to my other concerns, the loss of most or even all of the advantages I'd enjoyed for twenty years seemed a small matter. "I have a good education, and a good job, and hopes of an even better one."

He didn't say, "And besides, you're engaged to marry a wealthy young man." The fact that he didn't say it told me that my mother must have given him an anguished account of why Greg and I might never marry.

I said, "If I give you power of attorney, can you handle the sale of the duplex and the East Hampton house, as well as other financial matters?"

"Of course. But are you sure—"

"I'm sure. You see, I'm going to ask for a leave of absence and then go to Prosperity, New Mexico."

He looked appalled, "Debby, is that wise?"

"To me it seems the only course that makes sense. I'll want to see my father. Could you arrange that? I mean, I don't know anything about prisons. There may be a lot of red tape to be cut through."

After a moment he said, "Different prisons have different rules. I know nothing about that one. But if you plan to go to Prosperity first—"

"I do."

"Then the best thing would be to ask the local authorities right there where the crime was committed, to arrange for your visit. But Deborah, can't I persuade you to reconsider? It will be a grueling experience for you, especially so soon after your mother's—"

"I've thought it through, Mr. Greenwood. If possible, I'm going to fly out there day after tomorrow." I got to my feet and then said, "One thing more. Do you have

58

any idea whether or not my father knows that Mother—"

"He does. Since I was the one who handled the correspondence between him and your mother all these years, I sent him notification of her death. Well, good luck, Debby, in case I don't see you again before you leave."

Now, looking down into Prosperity's wide main street, I again saw Acting Chief of Police Ben Farrel. Accompanied by a dark-haired young man, probably the same one I had seen at the typewriter in police headquarters earlier that evening, he moved along the opposite sidewalk and entered a doorway. In the plate-glass window beside it a green neon sign, BARNEY'S BAR AND GRILL, winked on and off.

"Happy hangover!" I thought viciously, and fell to brooding about how he had treated me the day before.

CHAPTER
SEVEN

I HAD ARRIVED in Prosperity late the previous day after an eight-hour journey, which had included two plane changes. In Silver City I had rented a Datsun and driven south through a landscape—dry, sparsely vegetated earth, an occasional tumbleweed racing along the roadside, a flat tableland in the distance—which seemed familiar to me, although whether from countless movies or buried childhood memories I could not have said.

Around four o'clock I entered Prosperity and drove along its main street, a street so wide that cars parked diagonally at the curbs. About half the buildings were brick, the others frame. One brick building flew the American flag from its peaked roof and had the words "Town Hall" in gilt letters above its wide doorway. Big plate-glass windows flanked the entrance.

Less than half a block beyond the Town Hall stood the three-story Hotchkiss Hotel, also of brick, with its narrow wooden sign running from above the entrance to the roof. Without hesitation I turned into the parking lot beside it. At the car rental agency in Silver City the clerk had told me that Prosperity had only one hotel. When I asked if I should phone ahead for a reservation, he had laughed and said, "In that little burg? I'll bet that hotel hasn't been full even once in the last thirty years."

The hotel desk clerk himself had carried my suitcase up to this room, with its barbed-wire patterned wallpaper and its lingering aroma of long-dead cigars. When the clerk left I glanced at my watch. If I hurried, I'd still have time to freshen up and then walk back to the Town Hall before five.

In the bathroom I found to my relief that the shower worked properly and that the towels, although thin, were plentiful. I redressed, not in the navy blue pantsuit I'd worn since leaving New York that morning, but in a lighter-weight green sweater and skirt.

Then I hesitated. I knew that, in accordance with my promise, I should call Greg and give him the name of my hotel. But already feeling lonely and homesick, I was reluctant to call, lest the sound of his voice cause me to break down. Finally I compromised. I lifted the phone and asked the desk clerk to connect me with the nearest telegraph office.

With the wire sent, I left the hotel. As I passed a liquor store, a dry-cleaning shop, a variety store, I noticed that people stared at me. Strangers, obviously, were rare in this little town.

I turned in at the Town Hall entrance. Ahead of me stretched a long corridor. Its lights had not been turned on, and so I could not read the signs that, farther along, jutted from above doorways. But the door directly to my right bore the legend, "Mayor's Office. Miguel Acosta, Mayor." The lettering on the left-hand door read, "Police Headquarters, Benjamin Farrel, Chief of Police."

I felt thankful. In that chapter in the district attorney's book—that chapter which I had read so often I could almost recite it—he had mentioned Police Chief Benjamin Farrel. So he was still in office, the man who had assembled the evidence against my father. He probably had liked Joe Hartley. According to that district attorney, almost everyone had. Surely Benjamin Farrel would not only arrange an interview for me with my father; he also would sympathize with my urgent need to find some way, any way at all, of securing my father's vindication and release.

I opened the door and went in. Late afternoon light slanting through the plate-glass window showed me a thin, gray-haired woman standing with back turned to me at a row of filing cabinets against one wall. When I'd closed the door she turned around.

Her gaze, like that of the passersby on the street, was curious. "Can I help you?"

"Yes. I'd like to see Mr. Farrel."

"What name, please?"

"Channing. Deborah Channing."

"Wait just a moment."

She went to that inner door and, without knocking, opened it partway and said, "Deborah Channing to see you, Ben."

"Who?"

"Deborah Channing."

"All right. Send her in."

When I opened the door wide and walked in, I saw a man seated at a desk, a copy of *Sports Illustrated* in his hand, his booted ankles crossed on the desk's surface. Even sitting down he appeared tall. He looked at me over the top of the magazine. Then his feet hit the floor with a thump. He stood up. To judge just by his clothing, a tieless khaki shirt and khaki pants, he might have been almost anything, from a gas station attendant to a rancher. But on the khaki shirt was a very official-looking badge, a holstered revolver slanted along his right hip, and a pair of handcuffs dangled from a belt loop on his left side.

Still, I thought, there must be some mistake. This man—sandy-haired and with the sort of bony face so many southwestern men seem to have—could not have been more than thirty. His eyes also were like those of many Westerners—gray eyes with the look of someone used to gazing long distances. But now they were focused on me with an expression I found gratifying. After my almost three-thousand-mile trip, and all that had gone before it, it was comforting to see appreciation in a young man's eyes.

64

He said, "What can I do for you, Miss Chalmers?"

"Channing."

"I'm sorry."

"That's all right. I wanted to see Chief Farrel."

"I'm Chief Farrel. Or anyway, I'm acting chief, while he's laid up. You see, my father and I are both named Benjamin. Won't you sit down?"

I took the chair opposite him. When we were both seated I said, "I flew out here from New York today. I've come about—about Joseph Hartley."

The name seemed to mean nothing to him. But then, how old could he have been at the time of my father's trial? Nine? Ten? Not much more than that.

I added, "He's my father."

Ben Farrel looked puzzled. "I thought you said your name was—Oh, I see. You're married."

"No. But after her divorce, my mother went to New York. She married a man named Channing, and he legally adopted me. That all happened about twenty years ago."

A flicker in the gray eyes now, as if he were beginning to remember something.

65

I said, "My father is in the penitentiary near Las Cruces. He's serving a life sentence. They said—I mean, he was convicted of killing a little girl named Daisy McCabe."

His face became unreadable. "I remember now." Then, after a pause: "Why have you come to see me, Miss Channing?"

"I want to visit my father. A lawyer in New York said that if there's any red tape to be cut through, the authorities here in Prosperity might be helpful."

He said promptly, "Of course I can help." Was he, I wondered, eager to be of service? Or had he, scenting trouble, decided to get rid of me as soon as possible? He went on, "The assistant warden at the prison is an old friend of my father's. He can arrange for you to get in at any time, even though the regular visiting day isn't until later in the month. Now when would you like to go up there?"

"Day after tomorrow? That would give me time to rest up a little, and get my bearings."

"Day after tomorrow it is. I'll call the prison first thing in the morning."

"Thank you. And there's something else. I'd like to see your father."

"My father! I'm afraid that's impossible. As I told you, he's laid up. Anyway, why do you want to see him?"

"Because he gathered the evidence against my father, at least all the evidence up until the time of his arrest."

"And so?" His voice now, like his face, was expressionless.

Perhaps if I hadn't been so tired, not only from the journey but from all the strain before it, I might have expressed myself more tactfully. As it was I burst out, "I think the evidence may have been wrong! I think that someone, somewhere along the line, may have made a bad mistake."

"And you think it was my father?" His voice was cold now.

"It could have been. At least I should have a chance to talk to him."

"Look, Miss-Channing-from-New-York. My father's only a cop in a one-horse town, the same as I am. But he's a good cop. He wouldn't make a mistake, especially in a case involving the death of a little girl. And he wouldn't manufacture evidence just to make a name for himself the way I've heard of some big-city cops doing."

"I'm not accusing him of anything! I just want to talk to him.

"You can't. He's recovering from a stroke."

"Recovering? Then surely it wouldn't harm him to talk to me for a few—"

"I don't want him to run that risk."

My anger was rising. "Don't you have any understanding at all? Can't you imagine what it's like to—"

"You bet I don't understand! You wait twenty years, until my father's almost reached retirement age, and then you come out here and try to kick up—"

"I didn't wait twenty years! It wasn't until recently that I knew my father was in prison. I didn't know where he was. My mother wanted me to have a normal, happy—"

Because my voice had begun to shake, I broke off.

When Benjamin Farrel answered, his tone was more even. "Very well. I can understand your feeling. And I'll do what I can for you. I'll set up your visit to the prison. And if you have questions that I can answer, I'll be glad to do so. But I think that if you're wise you'll take the plane back to New York, just as soon as you've seen your father. You won't do yourself or anyone else any good, raking over a case the town would just as soon forget."

You bastard, I thought. When I first came in here you looked at me like a tomcat scenting catnip, but now you want to run me out of town.

Aloud I said, "There is one thing you can tell me right now. That house where my parents and I lived when I was a very little girl. Do you know where it is?"

"About five miles east of town. If you drove down here from Silver City, as I suppose you did—"

"Yes, in a rental car."

"Then you must have passed it. It's a little house set only a hundred feet or so back from the north side of the road. It's the only house along that stretch."

"Who owns it now?"

"I'm not sure. A man named Whitely owned it for a while. Maybe he bought it before your father went to trial. Later someone named Burrow owned it and tried to make a go of it as a turkey ranch. He gave up finally and went back East. I don't know who owns the place now. Maybe the county took it over for back taxes. Anyway, if you go out there you won't have to worry about trespassing charges. Nobody cares that much about the place."

"Thank you," I said coldly.

"Anything else I can help you with?"

"Not right now. Perhaps later on." Maybe that would tell him that I didn't intend to be pushed out of town before I was ready to leave. "Good-bye, Mr. Farrel."

Face rigid with displeasure, he stood up. "Good-bye, Miss Channing."

Back at the hotel I had dinner in the otherwise almost empty dining room. Pot roast and vegetables. The pot roast was better than I had expected, but the accompanying potatoes, carrots, and green beans were almost indistinguishable from each other except by color. Stopping at the desk to buy a copy of the *Luna County Press* (Prosperity had no newspaper of its own, the elderly night clerk explained), I went up to my room, read for a while, and then went to bed. The day clerk had been right about the room's quietness. No asthmatic whine from the elevator reached my ears. Only an occasional car drove past in the street below. I thought of that old gag about small towns rolling up the sidewalks by nine at night.

Then, just as I was drifting toward sleep, I heard loud male talk and laughter out in the hall. A door opposite mine opened and then banged shut. The voices, although diminished in volume, were still loud enough for me to gather that the purpose of the meeting was poker. So evidently Prosperity did have night life of a sort, or at least the men in the town did. The game went on for more than four hours. A bearer of something or other—food or drink or both—came along the hall at intervals, knocked loudly on the door opposite mine, was greeted boisterously by the poker players, and then went away. Sometimes there were stretches of silence broken only by the very faint sound of cards slapped on a table. I would feel hope that at last they were going to shut up and just *play*. Then I would hear the voice of one of them launch into a monologue which, I was sure, was a "story," one of those drawn-out jokes men love to tell. Already wincing, I would wait for the roar of laughter and the slap of palms against wood.

When the game finally broke up, I had reached that stage of exhaustion that threatens to preclude sleep. Dim light was gray at the window before I finally lost consciousness, only to be shocked awake by the ringing of the bedside phone.

"Good morning, Miss Channing." It was the voice of the acting chief of police. "I'm calling to tell you that you have an appointment to see your father at eleven A. M. tomorrow. Just give your name to the guards at the gate."

I looked at my watch. Seven after eight. Plainly Ben Farrel had called the prison as early as possible and then called me, hoping thus to forestall my visiting his office.

"Thank you." I restrained the desire to bang the phone down in his ear.

I called the desk and said that under no circumstance was I to be disturbed. Somehow after that, despite my anger with Ben Farrel, and despite the mingled anticipation and anxiety I felt at the thought of my impending visit to that prison, I managed to get back to sleep. I awoke a little past one and had a brunch of tomato juice and scrambled eggs and toast in the luncheonette a few doors from the hotel.

Then, following Ben Farrel's directions, I drove out to that little house, that lonely house with its sand-coated floors, and its scrap of Disney wallpaper clinging to the boards in the smallest bedroom and, beyond the window, that bare backyard where my father had planted a young tree, not knowing—oh, surely not knowing!—that still deeper in the earth lay the body of a child.

Now, still standing at the hotel room window, I again thought of that obviously Indian face, peering in at me through a shattered windowpane in that little house. Tomorrow morning, before I drove to the prison, I would call on Ben Farrel and tell him about that man. Yes, I thought, looking down at the bar into which he and his companion had disappeared, if Farrel thought he had seen the last of me he was badly mistaken.

CHAPTER
EIGHT

No POKER GAME disturbed my sleep that
night. Thus I awoke in plenty of time to
shower, have breakfast at the luncheonette,
and still reach the police station a little after
nine. Again the outer office was empty
except for the gray-haired woman. This
morning she sat at one of the room's three
desks, typing something on an ancient
manual upright. The look that leaped into
her hazel eyes behind their rimless glasses
told me that now she knew who I was.
Either she'd been able to hear my conversation with Farrel, or he had told her
about it afterward. In a town this small,
word must have spread rapidly. Probably
everyone knew that the daughter of the man
who'd been convicted of Daisy McCabe's

murder had come back here, after all these years.

She said, "Oh! Miss Har—I mean, Miss Channing. I guess you want to see Mr. Farrel."

"Yes, please."

"Just a moment." She crossed to the inner door, opened it, closed it behind her. After a few seconds she came back out. "He's on the phone, but you can go in."

I entered in time to hear him say into the phone, "I'll have to call you back." He hung up. Face remote, he got to his feet.

"Something more about your prison visit, Miss Channing?"

"No, not that."

With obvious reluctance he said, "Well, sit down." When we were both seated I said, "Yesterday afternoon I went out to that little house my father owned."

"Yes?"

"Someone else was there. He looked through one of the broken windows at me. When I walked toward him, he whirled around and ran."

"What did he look like?"

"I'd say he was an Indian, somewhere in his forties. But he wasn't wearing Indian jewelry or a hat with a feather or anything like that. Just a leather jacket and denim shirt and pants.''

Ben Farrel smiled. "That's Johnny Whitecloud. He's entirely harmless. Just retarded.''

"He may be harmless, but he must feel guilty about something. Why else should he have run off like that?''

"Maybe someone has bawled him out for looking in windows. You see, he thinks like a child. When you started toward him, maybe he thought he was in for another bawling out.''

"But what was he doing out there?''

"Johnny Whitecloud is apt to turn up almost anywhere. When he isn't working, he roams around as freely as a coyote.''

"Working! What sort of a job could a man like that—''

"He works for the Gainsworths. Lawrence Gainsworth has a big house in the hills west of town. Johnny does simple gardening jobs, window washing, things like that.''

Gainsworth, the man my mother had told me about, the rich man who lived alone except for his daughter. Although by now, I reflected, the daughter probably had been married for many years.

"His employer must pay him well," I said. "That leather jacket looked expensive and almost new."

"Probably a Christmas present from Mr. Gainsworth. You see, Johnny has lived with the Gainsworths nearly all his life. He was only two when his mother came to work there as a cook. When she died a couple of years later, Gainsworth sort of adopted Johnny. Not legally, but he's always seen to it that Johnny was well taken care of."

He paused and then asked, "Anything else you want to know?"

"Not right at the moment."

Again I intended for my answer to dampen any hopes he might have about me flying back East as soon as I'd seen my father, and I could tell by a certain flicker in his eyes that I had succeeded.

"Well, I'd better get going if I'm to reach the prison by eleven o'clock." I stood up.

He also got to his feet. "About your visit with your father. I hope it goes the way you want it to."

So he did have at least a little human feeling for someone besides Benjamin Farrel, Senior. Apparently he realized how stressful it might be for me to meet, inside prison walls, the father I had not seen since early childhood.

"Thank you," I said, and walked out.

It was a quarter of eleven when, after an uneventful drive north over a desert baking beneath the late winter sun, I caught my first glimpse of the prison, a few miles beyond the small town named Las Cruces. The sight of it surprised me, not because it looked so strange but because it looked so familiar with its high walls of some sort of gray stone, its iron gate, its guard towers where, even from a distance, blue-uniformed men were visible behind what must have been bulletproof glass. So at least in some visual respects they had been realistic, all those movies I'd seen in which desperate men, bodies caught in the glare of searchlights, succeeded or failed to climb walls like those ahead before chattering machine guns picked them off. Now the thought of such movies—in the past forgotten almost as soon as I turned off the TV set or walked out of the theater—made me feel nauseated. Had there been such escape attempts at this prison, and if so, had my father felt wretched enough to join them?

Two uniformed men, one middle-aged,

the other thirtyish, guarded the gates. The older man said when he had opened one half of the gate, "Okay, Miss Channing. Just pull over into the parking area."

I drove in. Against one wall of the prison yard stood a row of cars. I left the Datsun there and walked to the steel-barred entrance to the prison itself. A guard there, who appeared to be only a couple of years older than myself, said politely, even pleasantly, "You're here to see Joe Hartley, right?"

It must be, I thought, that in this dreary place, where each day was almost exactly like the one before, any tidbit of news was seized upon. I could imagine both the prisoners and the guards saying to each other, "You hear about Hartley? His kid's going to show up here, after twenty years!"

The guard pushed a button beside the gate. Soon a door beyond the steel door opened. The guard slid back the gate, and then I was inside the prison, following still another guard along a corridor flanked by closed office doors. An elderly prisoner in gray shirt and trousers, who didn't even look up as we passed, was pushing a waxer over the hall's linoleum. I could smell the wax, and some sort of disinfectant, and something else, perhaps the odor of human misery.

Then I was in a big room. Light from barred windows shone on the cement floor and on the barrier that bisected the room, a barrier made of wood to about waist height and of heavy plate glass from there to the ceiling. At the guard's direction, I sat in a chair drawn up to one of the metal grilles set in the glass.

He said, "You'll have half an hour, miss."

Heart pounding, dimly aware that a second guard stood several yards away against the wall, I waited.

A door on the other side of the barrier opened and, accompanied by still another guard, a man came into the room. Except for his blue eyes, he seemed to be all gray—gray uniform, gray face, gray hair. For the first time, I actually realized that the young father I dimly remembered was now past fifty. Yet I felt that even if I had met him on Fifth Avenue, I would have known he was my father. No doubt it was an illusion, but the feeling was there.

He sat down on the other side of the metal grille. I gave him a shaky smile, and he smiled back. For a moment we sat in silence, looking at each other. Then he said, "Hello, honey."

"Hello, Papa."

So that was what I had called him when I was very little. Until now, when the word slipped out so naturally, I hadn't known that. "My little Debby. You're beautiful, honey. You look like your mother."

My throat ached so much that for a moment I couldn't speak.

"Was your mother still beautiful when—"

"Yes, still beautiful. And Papa, she—she didn't suffer. That taxi knocked her unconscious, and she stayed that way until she died."

"I know. Her lawyer told me so in his letter about it. He also told me about that book you'd found."

He didn't have to tell me what book.

"Oh, Debby! I so prayed you'd never run across that book. I thought the chances were that you wouldn't. You were only about twelve when it came out."

"You read it when it was first published?"

"Yes. They'd put me to work in the library several months before the D.A.'s book arrived in a shipment. I still work in the library. Cushiest job in the joint." He smiled, a certain peacefulness in his blue eyes. I wondered how many years it had taken him to achieve a measure of serenity.

He said, "Your mother's letters told me all about you. The schools and summer camps you went to, and when you graduated from college, and that good job you got in Wall Street. Some of her last letters were just bubbling over with news about that fine young man of yours. Fine family, she said, and absolutely crazy about you."

Greg. I didn't want to talk to him about Greg unless I absolutely had to.

My father said, "I guess you'll be flying back to New York after you leave here."

I took a deep breath. "No, Papa. I didn't come to New Mexico just to see you. I came to get you out of prison."

He said, after a long moment, "To get me out! Oh, baby! You can't. Men sentenced to life on that sort of charge—well, they serve their sentence."

"You could get out if you were proved innocent."

"Oh, honey! There was just too much evidence. I think even that D.A. would have been glad if I could have proved my innocence. I think he sort of liked me. But I was found guilty.

"Now you go back East, Debby. Marry your young man. Send me lots of snapshots of you and him and my grandkids. And don't worry about me. I've not only got a good job here. I've got a regular correspondent who sends me books."

"Who's that, Papa?"

"Lawrence Gainsworth, a rich fellow who lives in the hills west of the town. I'd appreciate it, honey, if you called him before you go East."

"I'd like to call. You see, I already know about him."

"Yes, I guess you would have. Your mother must have told you how he loaned her money so she could take you to New York, as far as possible from all the—"

He broke off, and then said, "And when you leave this place I want you to go back to New York. And don't forget to send those snapshots!"

I realized then that I was going to have to tell him about Greg. "Papa, unless I can change things, there may not be any marriage or any grandkids, not mine and Greg's anyway."

"What do you mean?" A flinching look in his eyes told me he'd already guessed the answer to that.

It was one of the hardest things I'd ever done, but I told him. About the stunned dismay with which Greg had read that chapter in that paperback book. About our anguished agreement to shelve our marriage plans for a while. And, finally, about my decision to come out to New Mexico.

"So please help me, Papa. If not for your own sake, then for mine. Help me to get you out of here."

His face had seemed to turn grayer as I talked. "Oh, God!" he said. "The sins of the fathers. That's always seemed to me the most unjust— And it is even more unjust when there wasn't any—"

He broke off, and then said, in a dull voice, "It's hopeless, but all right, Debby. I'll do anything you want, tell you anything you want."

I tried to keep my voice steady. "Papa, there's something I have to ask, even though I'm sure of the answer. You're innocent, aren't you?"

"Yes, honey. I gave that poor little kid a lift a few times when I saw her out on the road hitchhiking. Each time she said her mother had sent her on an errand and told her to hitch her way, and I guess it was true. Her mother was that careless. But I never harmed Daisy in any way.''

''Do you have any idea who did kill her?''

''No idea at all.''

''But, Papa, you must have some idea! Her mother said that Daisy had kept prattling about somebody named Joe. You just couldn't have been the only man around there named Joe. It's one of the commonest names there are.''

''Oh, there were other Joes. There was one eighty-year-old man—Joseph Gaines or Garner or something like that—over in that religious colony where your mother was raised. There were several kids in the colony and in Prosperity itself named Joe. There was a Joe Watts who worked in the post office, even though he was in a wheelchair. He'd lost both legs in the Korean War. There were even two women in town, one named Josephine and one Joanna, who some people called Jo, or Josie. But nobody could have believed that any of them had done it. Besides, there was that other evidence against me.''

I thought of the other evidence. ''That pocket piece of yours, that nugget they found in the little girl's hand. Don't you have any idea where you lost it?"

He shook his head wearily. "I hadn't missed it until about a week before I was arrested, but it could have fallen through a hole in my jacket pocket Lord knows how long before I realized it was gone. It was an old denim jacket I wore for work, and I'd been doing odd jobs for everyone who asked me that spring, trying to make up for the run of bad luck I was having with the chickens. I could have lost it almost anywhere."

"Even out at that religious colony?"

"Yes. Those people don't like to seek outside help for anything. But a few weeks before Daisy disappeared a twister had flattened a building out there, and they'd had to call in workmen."

"I don't even know where that colony is."

"Maybe you haven't been west of town. About three miles outside Prosperity there's a side road with a sign, or at least there used to be. It says, 'Beersheba, 4 miles.' Beersheba is what they call the place where they set up the colony."

After a moment I said, "Tell me about that—that tree."

"There's not much to tell. Your mother

had often talked about having a tree close to the house. And we both thought of how nice it would be to plant a good-sized sapling, so that in two or three years it would be big enough for me to put up a swing for you—"

He broke off abruptly, as if his throat had closed up. Then he said, "Anyway, I did some carpenter work for a guy who had a turkey ranch about fifteen miles from our place. He had a nice grove of cottonwoods, and he offered me a young tree. He said he and his son would ball the tree and drop it off at my place the next time they drove past. Better have the hole already dug, he told me, so that I could get it into the ground as soon as possible.

"I dug the hole, and put a little wire and stake fence around it so you wouldn't fall in. Then, three days after that, I had a bit of good luck. A guy I knew had gotten a job at a new resort up near Carlsbad Caverns. The manager wanted to have a couple of hundred chickens deep frozen, and my friend had persuaded him to buy from me. All I had to do was deliver them.

"Your mother got all excited. She'd never been to Carlsbad Caverns. Besides, we'd never had a honeymoon, so we decided this

87

would be it." He smiled. "Some honeymoon, I guess. Bride and groom and three-year-old kid and a truckload of squawking chickens. But we figured it would be great. I left a note for the turkey rancher, saying that he could just put the tree in the backyard and I'd plant it the minute I got back. I also arranged for this Indian guy, Johnny Whitecloud—not very bright but reliable enough—to feed and water the chickens we still had."

He paused. "Do you remember anything at all about that trip to Carlsbad?"

I shook my head.

"No, I suppose not. But you seemed to love it, all of it, even the Caverns. You didn't scream and yell and have to be taken out, the way some kids older than you did. Anyway, we'd planned to be gone only three days but it turned out to be four. The truck's engine conked out, and we had to wait for a part to arrive from Roswell. When we got home, the cotton sapling was in the backyard. Even though it was past sunset, I planted the tree and watered it and filled in the hole and tamped the dirt down. I remember feeling a little surprised at the size of the hole I'd dug. It was larger than I'd needed. But I didn't think much about it.''

Bleakness came into his face and voice. ''The next day in town I learned that Daisy McCabe's mother, Loretta, had reported her little girl missing. In fact, the child had been missing for a couple of days before her mother reported it. She'd figured Daisy had just run off to her cousin's house near Bolton, the county seat, the way she had a few times before. But finally, while you and your mother and I were at the Caverns, she went to Ben Farrel, the chief of police.''

Again he paused, and then said with a rush, ''The second day after you and your mother and I got home, Ben Farrel came out there with a deputy and a search warrant. They dug up the tree and found Daisy, three or four feet below its roots. She'd been strangled, and she had that nugget of mine clenched in her hand.''

He fell silent. The guard standing against the wall on my side of the barrier cleared his throat, and I wondered if it was a warning that my half hour was almost up. I said hurriedly, ''But you and Mother and I had been away! How could they think that you—''

''They figured that I'd killed her and then buried her before we left for the Caverns.

As for the tree, the D.A. said that indicated premeditation. I'd known I was going to do that terrible thing, and so I'd asked that turkey farmer for the tree so that I'd have an excuse to—to get the hole ready.

"Oh, the D.A. himself admitted that there were weak points in the case against me. For instance, how had I dared to go away with the tree not yet in place over —over the little girl's grave? But murderers often showed that kind of overconfidence, he said, only he used a Greek word, *hubris*.

"And, anyway, there was all the evidence against me. Loretta McCabe saying that Daisy had kept talking about her friend Joe. All the people who'd seen Daisy in the truck with me at various times. And then her being found, with my nugget in her fist, beneath a tree I'd planted in my own backyard. As the D.A. said, many men had been hung on far less evidence than that."

I sat silent, struggling with a sense of hopelessness. My father said, "They told me it was Ben Farrel who'd arranged for you to visit me, even though it isn't visiting day. So he's still chief of police."

"Yes. But it was his son who arranged the visit. The Ben Farrel you knew had a stroke, and his son is now acting chief."

He shook his head wonderingly. "Little Benjy, chief of police! He was only eight or nine years old the last time I saw him. Even then he was planning to join his dad's police force when he grew up. Well, I guess he did."

After a moment he said gently, "You see how hopeless it is, don't you, Deborah?"

Unable to speak, I shook my head.

"Oh yes you do. Go back to New York, honey. Tell that young fellow all I've told you today. If he really loves you, and I don't see how he could help it, he'll marry you.

"And try not to worry about me. I've—adjusted. Life could be a lot worse than I've found it in here." He paused. "Maybe you've heard that the one kind of convict the other cons are tough on is a child murderer."

Still unable to speak, I nodded.

"It hasn't been that way for me. Oh, it was at the very first. But soon they decided I couldn't have done it."

His fellow prisoners were convinced he was innocent. I knew he was, and he knew it, and yet unless I could find him—that man, probably named Joe, who had killed and then seemingly vanished into thin air—my father was going to be shut up in this place until he died.

"So go on back, little one," he said, "go on back to where you grew up safe and beautiful and happy."

"Time's up, young lady." Until the guard said that, I had not realized he had walked over to stand beside me.

I said, "No, Papa. I'll see you the next visiting day, if not before."

"Please, honey! Please! Don't stay out here."

I shook my head.

"Come on, miss! Time's up."

I put my palm against the glass. My father, trying to smile, placed his palm on the other side of the glass. Then I shoved my chair back and hurried toward the door.

CHAPTER
NINE

I DROVE SOUTH and west over sandy earth that, except for an occasional arroyo, seemed almost as flat as a billiard table. Each spring after the first rain, my mother had told me, a miracle happened here in this arid land. Almost overnight, wild flowers whose seeds lay dormant for all but a few weeks of the year would rise up along the mesquite and cacti, so that the vast sandy waste looked like a many-hued Persian carpet. But now the landscape appeared almost as lifeless as the moon's surface. Through some trick of the afternoon light, distant mesas, reddish in color, seemed to float above the desert floor.

I gave only vague attention to the landscape or to the occasional cars I passed. All my thoughts were concentrated on that gratifying and yet painful reunion with my father. I kept going over and over the evidence against him, evidence so strong that I could understand how the jury, however reluctantly, had pronounced him guilty. But he hadn't been. I was absolutely sure of that now. Someone else had killed Daisy, perhaps someone whose name was Joe. And yet no one else of that name had seemed even remotely suspect, not the legless Joseph who had worked in the post office, nor the eighty-year-old Joseph in that religious colony—

That colony. There was little chance that the octogenarian of twenty years ago would still be alive. But there would be others out there who remembered my mother and father, remembered Daisy McCabe. Maybe by talking to them I could learn something that would help. It was a forlorn hope, but I had no choice except to grasp at any hope.

I'd go out there right away, I suddenly resolved. There were still several hours of daylight left.

By now I was passing the houses on Prosperity's outskirts, drab little houses of faded stucco mainly, although here and there stood a small ranch-style house, probably prefabricated, and certainly of more recent vintage than its neighbors. Then I was moving down wide Main Street past the bank, the gas station, the Town Hall—I could see no one at all behind the police station's plate-glass window—the luncheonette, the hotel. I didn't stop there, but drove out of town and kept on going west, toward that line of low hills. After about three miles I saw the side road my father had mentioned. The arrow-shaped sign, "Beersheba, 4 miles," was there, too, but it looked so new that I doubted it was the same one my father remembered. Probably the colonists replaced the sign at intervals.

As I turned onto the dirt side road—narrow, but in better shape than the asphalt county road I had left—I found myself feeling a certain anticipation. Whether or not I learned anything from these people, I would at least see the place where my mother had lived all her life, until the elders had been incautious enough to send her out to work in that diner. Suddenly I realized that I had seen no diner in Prosperity. Probably it had long since gone out of business.

Ahead now, stretching away from both

sides of the road, were lines of tall junipers, obviously planted as windbreaks. In this arid landscape their greenness was welcome to the eye. I crossed a wooden bridge over a narrow ravine. Then I was beyond the windbreaks and in another world, a kind of miniature Imperial Valley. I saw irrigation ditches, fed by water gushing from huge cement pipes, on either side of the road. Beyond the ditches stretched lush fields of tomato, lettuce, green peppers, green beans, and other plants I did not recognize. Farther away, a line of greenhouses glittered in the sun.

Both men and women moved between the fields' neat rows, some cultivating with hoes, others picking vegetables and placing them carefully in canvas bags slung from one shoulder. The men wore overalls and shirts and broad straw hats, the women dark dresses and the sort of cloth sunbonnets you see in faded old photographs. Evidently the colonists were used to visitors, because the workers in the fields looked up only briefly as I passed.

Ahead were buildings on both sides of the road. As I drew closer I saw to my surprise that the colonists had adopted the native Indian architecture, flat-roofed, two-story structures of brown adobe. Then I realized that such construction, however incongruous with overalls and sunbonnets, had been a sensible choice. The Southwest's adobe buildings, I had read somewhere, afforded warmth during the few weeks of relatively cold weather each winter, and cool shelter from the blazing sun the rest of the year.

I drove slowly down the wide dirt street, past an adobe building with the one word "Store" painted in neat black letters above its wide doorway. Next to it was a larger building. Through its open windows on the ground floor came the sound of treble voices reciting in unison. This, I realized, must be the Children's Building, where children from five to fourteen, my mother had told me, not only attended classes on the first floor but, on the second, slept in strictly supervised dormitories. The structures on the other side of the street, I knew, included the Men's Building and the Women's Building, where children under five also were housed, and the Connubial Building, where married couples were allowed to spend a night together once a week. But which building was which I had no idea. At the end of the street, set at right angles to the other buildings, was another structure with a wide doorway. The sound of saws and hammers issued from it. There must have been a big skylight in its roof, because I could see overalled men moving about. This apparently was where the colonists made classically simple chairs and tables and benches, not only for their own needs but for sale to the outside world.

I made a U-turn and started back along the street. No pedestrians moved along the wooden sidewalks. Evidently at this mid-afternoon hour everyone was occupied, either in the fields, or the furniture factory, or the school. I parked in front of the store and went inside.

Displayed on the wall to my left were two patchwork quilts, one of red background and one of blue. Both had been worked in the wedding ring pattern. On the opposite wall, ladder-back, rush-bottomed chairs hung from pegs. Facing me across a counter sat a woman who appeared to be in her sixties, her dark hair streaked with gray, her expression composed. She was knitting something that looked like the sleeve of a child's red sweater. The counter displayed, in small straw baskets, cherry tomatoes and green peppers and purple grapes, all of them, I imagine, from the colony's green-houses. Through an archway beside her I could see a tall, bearded man standing at a workbench. With a small brush he was applying some sort of finish—a varnish to judge by the smell of it—to the leg of a ladder-back chair.

"Good afternoon." The woman's voice was polite but aloof. "May I help you?"

"I'd like a basket of grapes, please."

"Pick any basket you like. They're two dollars each."

I gave her the money, drew one of the baskets toward me, and then hesitated. She asked, "Will there be anything else?"

"No, thank you. But may I ask you something?" As she looked at me with calm gray eyes, neither refusing nor assenting, I said, "Have you been here long, Mrs.—"

"Mrs. Jenkins, Naomi Jenkins. I was born here."

"Then you must remember my father, or at least remember hearing about him. His name was Joseph Hartley."

Blankness in her gaze for a moment, and then an odd mixture of sympathy and re-pulsion. "Yes. I remember. He was—he was put away because of Daisy McCabe."

"Yes. But he didn't kill that child, Mrs.

Jenkins, and I need terribly to find out who did do it."

Striding footsteps. Then the bearded man stood in the doorway. It wasn't the sort of beard worn by West Coast movie directors and East Coast Madison Avenue types. A mottled gray and black, and straggling to the middle of his chest, it gave him an almost frightening aspect. To judge by photographs, God's Angry Man, John Brown, looked like that.

"Who is this, Wife?"

Until now I had thought that only husbands in nineteenth-century novels used that form of address.

Nervousness in her eyes now, although her voice remained calm. "It's Joseph Hartley's daughter, Samuel."

He gazed at me from surprisingly bright gray eyes, deep-set beneath thick brows. "You had best just go away and forget him, girl, him and that Daisy McCabe too. They both deserved everything that happened to them."

Struck dumb, I looked at him. I could see how he might feel that way about my father, a man who, however unjustly, had been convicted of an atrocious crime. But to feel like that about a slain child!

100

"Young as she was, she was a wanton and a temptress. She ran loose all over the place. She even came here several times." He turned and pointed a gnarled finger into his workroom. "Right there, right while I was sitting at my workbench one day, she came in and leaned up against my side and put her hand on my knee. She was pretending to be interested in my work, but she didn't fool me. I know an instrument of the devil when I see one. I told her to be gone, and she ran out."

Still speechless, I wondered if Daisy McCabe could possibly have been an incipient Lolita. I rejected the idea. It was far, far more likely that the lonely and neglected child had hoped to gain a little adult attention and approval by showing an interest in his work. Her innocent gesture had evoked feelings in Samuel Jenkins, a sexually repressed man of perhaps forty-odd, feelings that horrified him so much that he could accept no responsibility for them. Only the child, "the devil's instrument," was guilty, so guilty that she had deserved to die.

"Go on back where you came from, young woman. Sufficient to that time was the evil thereof."

I urged myself to feel tolerant of this aging fanatic, but I could not keep from saying, "You have no right to—" I broke off. After all, there was something more I needed to know.

"Very well. I'll leave in a few moments. But first I'd like to ask about a man named Nathaniel Crisp. Is he still here?"

The deep-set eyes studied me. The silence lengthened. Then Mrs. Jenkins said, "Yes, Brother Nathaniel is still here. He's in charge of the furniture shop." The nervous smile she gave me told me that although she probably would never acknowledge it to anyone, even herself, she was embarrassed by her husband's behavior.

He said, "What business could you have with Brother Nathaniel, girl? Or is it your mother who wants news of him? Well, you tell her that Brother Nathaniel has been thankful for many years now that Providence saved him from marrying her. He has a fine, God-fearing wife and three obedient and respectful children. You tell her that."

I did not answer that my mother was dead. I was afraid he would say that her death was God's judgment upon her. Instead I said, "Very well. I'll drive down to the furniture shop and—"

"Oh no you won't! I'll give you no chance to flaunt yourself before those men, some of them even younger than you are." I had a sudden, weird sensation that I was dressed, not in a quite ordinary brown-and-white striped shirtwaist dress, but in the wispiest of bikinis. "If you must speak to Brother Nathaniel, I'll send him back here." He strode out onto the wooden sidewalk.

So actually he did want to know what had brought me here. Unwilling to admit his curiosity to me, he hoped to learn more about my purpose from Brother Nathaniel.

I said to Mrs. Jenkins, "I'll wait in my car."

"Don't forget your grapes." As I drew the basket toward me she added, "If my husband seems harsh, it is only because God has directed him to smite sin root and branch wherever he finds it. But he is a good man, a fine man."

Perhaps. Perhaps they were all good people. Certainly they were industrious. They indeed had made the desert blossom as a rose. And probably all the children, not just Brother Nathaniel's, were obedient and respectful of their elders, creating none of the problems that plagued schools in the world outside. I found it impossible to picture teenagers in this colony sneaking out into the fields to experiment with drugs.

Still, there seemed to be an oppressiveness in the very air here. And now that I had met Samuel Jenkins, a man capable of regarding a lonely eight-year-old as a sexual wanton, I could realize that my mother must have been pleased indeed when the financially distressed colonists sent her to work in that diner.

I gave Mrs. Jenkins a noncommittal nod and a polite good-bye and went out to sit in the Datsun. Samuel Jenkins did not return to the store, at least not while I was there, but after a few moments an overalled man emerged from the furniture shop and walked rapidly toward me. Like Jenkins, he was tall and thin and dark-haired, but he wore no beard. He stopped beside the car. He was much younger than Jenkins, I saw now, and rather handsome in a dark, gaunt sort of way.

"You wanted to see me?" I could tell from the look in his eyes, almost a look of recognition, that he thought I resembled my mother. I could also tell from his expression, bitterness strangely touched with longing, that despite the God-fearing wife and three obedient children he had never forgotten my mother. Nor forgiven her.

"It's about my father. My mother told me that after she married him you came out to that little chicken ranch. I guess that was quite a while before my father was arrested, but just the same I—I wondered if you have any idea who killed that little girl."

"The jury said Joe Hartley did it."

"But he didn't! I saw my father just this morning, and I'm absolutely sure he couldn't have done it. It was someone else—"

I broke off. His eyes, so dark blue they were almost black, had become as expressionless as glass. I said, "Can you remember anyone named Joe, someone Daisy McCabe might have known?"

"There were lots of Joes, but Joe Hartley was the only one among them who could have done it. Besides, the court had only Loretta McCabe's word for it that her little girl kept talking about a man named Joe." He paused. "Have you talked to Loretta McCabe?"

"Not yet." I had shrunk from the idea of meeting the mother of that little girl.

"Well, I doubt if it would be much use to see her. She's not just a harlot. She's a drunkard, too, like that man she lives with. In your place, I'd try to put the whole thing out of my mind. I guess that's what your mother tried to do when she left here about twenty years ago." He added, after a moment. "Is your mother out here with you?"

"No. My mother is dead."

His face went rigid. "How?"

I told him.

Again a strange expression in his eyes, a blend of triumph and pain. He did not say, as I had feared Samuel Jenkins might, that it was the Lord's judgment upon my mother. But I could tell he was thinking it.

He said, "Unless you've got something more to ask, I'd like to get back to work."

I wanted to say, "Don't you know anything, anything at all, that might help my father?" But that would have been absurd. Why should he want to help? If Nathaniel Crisp still felt bitter toward my mother for eluding him, how much more bitter must he feel toward the man who had married her?

I said, "All right, Mr. Crisp. Thank you."

He walked away. I made a U-turn in the wide street and drove back along the road between the beautifully cultivated fields.

CHAPTER
TEN

IT WAS LATE afternoon by the time I stopped in the hotel parking lot and then, carrying my basket of grapes, went around to the lobby. A tall man in khaki got up from one of the worn leather chairs.

"Hello, Miss Channing." This time his manner was almost friendly.

"Hello, Mr. Farrel."

His eyes had gone to the basket of grapes. I could tell from his expression that he knew they came from Beersheba, but all he said was, "Could we talk for a moment? I thought we might go to the luncheonette and have some coffee."

"All right. First I'd better take these grapes up to my room."

"You can leave them here at the desk,

Miss Channing," the clerk said, "and pick them up later."

"Thank you."

Ben Farrel and I went outside. The sun was low now. The Gainsworth house up on the crest of the hills was silhouetted against pinkish clouds. Almost level rays of bronze-colored sunlight illumined the little town's main street. We went into the luncheonette and sat in a booth next to the plate-glass window. A red-haired waitress of about twenty-five came from behind the counter and walked over to us, order pad in hand. She gave me a look, curious and a little hostile, and then turned to my companion. "Hello, Ben. How's it going?"

Her tone was flirtatious. Well, that wasn't surprising. Ben Farrel was attractive, if you like the roughhewn, taciturn type.

"Can't complain, Nancy. How's yourself?"

His smile was frankly appreciative of her pretty although heavily made-up face. I became sure then that he was single. In a tiny town like this, a married man might respond to a girl like Nancy, but not quite in that straightforward way.

"I'm fine," Nancy said. "What'll it be, folks?"

"Coffee, please."

"The same for me," Ben said.

When she had brought our cups and then gone back to the counter, he said, "You saw your father?"

"Yes."

"And?"

What was he hoping? That my father, confronted by his grown daughter, had admitted his guilt?

I said evenly, "Yes, I saw him. And I'm more convinced than ever that he did not kill that child."

"Did he suggest some other suspect?"

No discernible irony in his tone, but I still had the feeling it was there. "No."

"You also went to Beersheba today?"

"Yes."

"Learn anything?"

"Not really." Only that a self-appointed instrument of the Almighty out there told me that both my father and that eight-year-old child deserved their fate. Only that a man who wanted to marry my mother had been so devastated over losing her to another man that now, after a quarter of a century, his bitterness was still there.

"Look, Deborah." I wondered if he realized that he had called me by my given name. "Suppose that by some wild chance you are right. Suppose someone else was guilty, someone who is still around here. Don't you realize you might be in danger, wandering about all by yourself?"

I said dryly, "Are you offering me a police escort?"

"Scarcely. As chief, my father had three deputies, one of them me, and was short-handed. I've got only two deputies, so I'm even more shorthanded."

"Oh, dear! And so much crime to cope with here in Prosperity!"

"You'd be surprised, Miss Channing, at the amount of trouble we do have here." So I was Miss Channing again. "Not just the usual Saturday night brawls and the occasional rapes or robberies. Several times motorcycle gangs have come here with the notion that it might be fun to take a little town like this apart. And always there are drugs coming over the border. Sometimes drivers try to sneak it on back roads through small towns. I don't imagine we succeed in confiscating one batch out of five, but we try."

"And since I'm just so much extra trouble, you want me to leave?"

"Yes, but not just for that reason.

110

You're wasting your time here. And then there's my father. I still don't want him upset. He hasn't yet heard about your being out here, but I can't keep it from him forever."

"Why should he be so upset over the idea of my questioning the evidence?"

"Because he's a sick man! And sick men have tender egos. He won't like the idea of your trying to prove he overlooked something. He won't even like being reminded of the McCabe case. It was an especially painful one for him."

Could it be that Daisy had been related to the Farrels? I asked apprehensively, "Why especially painful?"

"Because he liked Joe Hartley so much. He always had a smile and a little joke for everyone. He never shortweighted anybody who bought his chickens. When he was called in for a plumbing job or carpentry or some such, he always showed up on time and did a good job. Kids liked him too. Certainly I did. When I was eight he gave me a bantam hen about a third the size of a Rhode Island Red. I called her Eunice, and trained her to ride behind me on my bicycle. I was the only kid in town with a midget hen for a pet. She lived for a long time. She was still alive several years after Joe Hartley—" He broke off.

I pictured him, a freckled-faced kid— surely with that sandy hair he'd had freckles —riding around town with Eunice. I liked the picture. In fact, because of the things he'd just said about my father, I found myself liking him a little—but just a little, not enough to oblige him by leaving town.

I said, "If you and everyone else liked my father, how is it any of you could have believed he committed that terrible crime?"

"Evidence is evidence. If you decided cases on how well liked the accused had been, a lot of criminals would go scot-free. You know how it is when someone's arrested for a violent crime. A neighbor will say, 'A nicer, politer man I've never met.' His pastor will say, 'He's been in church nearly every Sunday, and he sees to it that his children are in Sunday School.' His boss will say, 'I'd have trusted him further than any employee I ever had.' And so on, and so on. Evidently a guy can really be like that, and then suddenly something goes wrong inside his head—"

I remained silent, not in the least convinced.

After a moment he said, "Who are you

going to see next?"

"Daisy McCabe's mother."

"You won't find that very pleasant."

Not very pleasant. Neither was a life sentence to prison very pleasant. I shrugged.

Suddenly he sounded tired. "Well, if I can't convince you—" He looked at his watch. "I'd better get back to the office."

We walked out into dazzling sunset light. I thanked him for the coffee, and he nodded. Then he turned toward police headquarters, and I turned toward the hotel.

CHAPTER
ELEVEN

I COLLECTED MY basket of grapes from the desk clerk and went up to my room. After that dusty ride over the dirt road from the highway to Beersheba and back I felt in need of a shower. But first, I decided, I would phone Lawrence Gainsworth. A later call might disturb his dinner hour. From the lower shelf of the telephone stand beside the bed I picked up the phone book, which listed not only Prosperity's phones but those of this whole sparsely settled county. I looked up the Gainsworth number and then asked the desk clerk to connect me.

A woman with a Mexican accent answered the phone. I said, "This is Deborah Channing. May I speak to Mr. Gainsworth?"

He came on the line a few moments later. "Hello, there!" His voice was pleasant, and much younger sounding than I had expected. "I heard you were out here."

"I imagine everyone has heard that by now. After all your kindnesses to my mother and my father and me, I know I should have called you before this. But I wanted to see my father first."

"And have you seen him?"

"Yes. Today."

"I'd like to hear about your visit with him, or at least as much as you'd care to tell me."

"I'd be very glad to tell you about it."

He said, after a moment, "I know this is very short notice indeed. But would you have dinner with my daughter and me tonight at our house?"

"I'd like that very much indeed." I not only welcomed the prospect of meeting the man who had befriended my parents. I also welcomed a respite from the hotel's vegetables.

"Would half an hour be enough time for you to get ready?" When I said it would, he went on, "I'll send the car for you."

"Oh, Mr. Gainsworth. That won't be necessary."

"It would be best. At night you might miss the turnoff to our house. I'd drive into town myself to get you if I weren't waiting for an important phone call."

In record time I showered, put on the best dress I'd brought with me, a pale-pink silk chemise, picked up a knitted gray shawl, and went down to the lobby to wait. I hoped that the car would not be driven by Johnny Whitecloud. Probably it would not be. Probably someone like him would not be able to obtain a driver's license. And anyway, it seemed unlikely that Mr. Gainsworth would send a retarded man to chauffeur a guest.

He did not. The thin young man who, wearing a dark-blue suit, walked into the lobby was obviously of Mexican ancestry. He walked over to where I sat. "Miss Channing? I'm Enrique, Mr. Gainsworth's driver."

We went out into the early dark. The car I entered was not the Lincoln or Mercedes I had envisioned, but an unassuming Buick, or Oldsmobile, I was not sure which. We drove along the level highway for a few miles and then began to climb. It was strange how only a few feet of elevation could make a difference in the native

116

vegetation. On the desert floor almost the only trees were those planted by man. But soon we were driving among evergreens interspersed with broadleaf trees, and then through solid stands of pine. After the dry desert air, I found the cool, pine-scented dark pleasant.

The car turned off onto a side road, a narrow dirt one but well kept up, with no potholes or gullies. We rounded a curve, and there was the house, its square turrets dimly visible against the night sky. Light shone from its long first-floor windows and through the wrought iron grille, which guarded its glass front door.

Lawrence Gainsworth himself admitted me to the house. Gray-haired and handsome, he stood there on the red-tiled floor of the entrance hall and, smiling at me, extended his hand, with his elbow still bent, a little away from his body. It was an awkward gesture. As we shook hands he said, in explanation, "I broke my arm in three places a long time ago, and it never healed properly."

"Oh, dear! A car accident?"

"No, a horse threw me. I broke not only my arm but my collarbone. But let's talk about you. How very much you look like your mother, Deborah. You don't mind my calling you that, do you? After all, I knew you when you were an infant."

"Of course I don't mind."

"Come into the library and meet my daughter."

We went through an archway into a room lined almost solidly with books. Many of them had calf bindings that gleamed faintly in the mingled lamplight and the glow of a small fire burning beneath a black marble mantel. A thin, dark-haired woman of forty-odd, dressed in a green silk caftan, got up from a chair beside the fireplace and walked toward us, smiling tentatively. I saw that she was perhaps two or three inches taller than myself. My mother had described Rachel Gainsworth as "quite attractive, but frail-looking and very shy." I gained an impression the description still fitted.

"Deborah, this is my daughter, Rachel."

She said, in a soft, musical voice, "It's very nice to meet you, Deborah."

Lawrence Gainsworth opened a mahogany liquor cabinet and served our drinks, sherry all around. We sat beside the fireplace, Rachel Gainsworth and I on a Victorian love seat upholstered in brown velvet, her father in a high-backed chair upholstered in the same material. Through an archway I could see part of a dimly lighted living room. Evidently there the furniture was a blend of Victorian and eighteenth century, because I could see a pair of what looked like Duncan Phyfe side chairs flanking a high-backed Victorian sofa upholstered in red brocade.

Lawrence Gainsworth said, "If you'd rather not talk to us about your visit with your father, I'm not going to hold you to it, Deborah."

"I don't mind talking about it. Of course in some ways it was disturbing." My throat tightened at the thought of my first glimpse of that man who was all gray now, except for those oddly serene blue eyes. After a moment I was able to go on. "But in another way my visit with him was very gratifying."

Mr. Gainsworth said, "Gratifying?"

"Yes, because I became more convinced than ever that someone else killed Daisy McCabe."

He nodded. "Of course someone else killed her."

His quick agreement caught me by surprise. After a moment I said eagerly, "How do you know? Do you have any idea who really—"

"Deborah, forgive me. I didn't mean to get your hopes up. All I meant was that in spite of all the evidence against him, I never believed your father was guilty. I find it simply impossible to think of your father killing anyone, let alone a child."

I felt a crushing disappointment. For a moment I'd thought that perhaps he had some proof of my father's innocence. But of course he could not have had that. If he had, he long ago would have tried to secure my father's release. And anyway, it had been comforting to hear his assessment of my father's character.

Rachel made her first contribution to the conversation. She said to me, with a shy smile, "Your father is so nice. Once my car stalled on the road near his house. He came out and fixed it." She added, oddly, "I used to drive in those days."

Why *used* to drive? Did her thinness and her pale, almost transparent skin mean that she had some sort of progressive illness, something that no longer permitted her to drive?

Mr. Gainsworth said, "That was the day you sketched the hen and baby chicks, wasn't it?"

"Yes." Again she turned to me with that shy smile. "Your mother came out to where he was working on my car. She had you in her arms. I guess you were only a few months old then. She mentioned that one of the hens had hatched out chicks that day and I asked if I could go back to the nesting box and make a sketch."

Lawrence Gainsworth said, "She's come a long way as an artist since then. In those days I didn't realize what a talented child I had."

"Oh, Father!"

"No false modesty now, Rachel. You know you're good. After dinner we'll show your work to Deborah, and she can judge for herself. And speaking of dinner—"

He looked at the wide-banded gold watch encircling his wrist. Poignantly I was reminded of Greg, not just by the watch itself, the same make as Greg's, but by the brown wrist it encircled and the impeccable white cuff above. "Yes, surely it's time for—"

A gong sounded softly somewhere nearby.

We walked back along the tile-floored hall to the dining room. Here, too, the furniture was Victorian, a massive mahogany sideboard and a long mahogany table, lit by candles set in elaborate silver candelabra. Probably, I reflected, this furniture had been bought by Lawrence Gainsworth's grandfather who, when near his old age, had built this house.

But there was nothing stodgy or Victorian about the paintings on the walls. They shimmered with color. A Monet landscape. Two Georgia O'Keeffe still lifes. An early Picasso clown. A red-haired Toulouse-Lautrec demimondaine, long cigarette holder poised. If these were originals—and I could scarcely imagine him hanging reproductions—then there was a fortune in art in this room. I caught him watching me with amusement, as if he guessed what I was thinking.

He said, "Except for the O'Keeffes, I bought these paintings in Paris when I was a very young man."

"They're lovely."

Dinner was served by a thin Mexican woman who might have been Enrique's mother. She bore a facial resemblance to the chauffeur. Apparently she was also the cook, because when I praised the baby lamb chops and peas and stuffed potatoes, Lawrence raised his voice and said, "Miss

Channing likes your food, Consuelo."

The woman beamed. When she had gone out he said, "Consuelo is quite deaf, but she reads lips well."

During the first part of the meal I was aware of the awkwardness with which my host, because of that long-ago injury, manipulated his knife. But there was nothing awkward about his conversation. He spoke entertainingly of New Mexico's history—the cattle driven along the old Chisholm Trail, the warfare between cattlemen and sheepmen, and, toward the end of the nineteenth century, the opening up of the silver mines by his own forebears.

Later the talk turned to books. We exchanged opinions (favorable) about Barbara Tuchman's new book and (unfavorable) about the latest four-pound opus of an oft-married writer so flamboyant that he made Hemingway look like a cloistered monk.

Both her father and I tried to draw Rachel into the conversation. It was no use. She would answer with a mere yes or no or, sometimes, "I really haven't thought about it."

How strange, I thought, that a man of Lawrence Gainsworth's cultivation should live out his life up here in these hills above that little town. The only reason I could think of for his remaining here was his daughter's health. Perhaps doctors had advised him that she needed southern New Mexico's dry climate. If so, it was sad for him, but even sadder for her. Despite her more than comfortable surroundings, it must be a bleak life indeed for an attractive and still youngish woman.

Now Mr. Gainsworth was talking about a box of books he had just received from a New York secondhand bookseller. "One of the books is an out-of-print edition of Hazlitt's essays. I ordered it so I could send it to your father."

"My father, reading Hazlitt!"

"Why, yes. He's become interested in Hazlitt of late."

I knew from my mother that my father had not gone beyond high school. And I had never gathered from her that he had any sort of literary bent. I said, "When did he start becoming interested in books?"

"Oh, it must have been many years ago. All I'm sure of is that I sent him some novels—Jack London's, if I remember correctly—before he'd been in prison a year. He wrote back that he'd enjoyed them, so I sent him more, both fiction and nonfiction. Then he transferred from the machine shop to the prison library, which brought him into contact with many books.''

After a moment he added gently, ''As I'm sure you know, Deborah, many men have gained an education in prison. A few of them, from John Bunyan to Eldridge Cleaver, have become writers while behind bars. So, terrible as it is to think of your father imprisoned for something that you don't believe he did and I don't believe he did, his situation could be much worse. As long as he has books, he can travel in his mind. Thank God, no one has ever invented a way of imprisoning a mind.''

I felt he was speaking of himself as well as my father. Lawrence Gainsworth, although kept here because of his daughter's frail health or because of some circumstance I did not know about, could also ''travel in his mind.''

I said, ''Yes, I realize that books must be a blessing for anyone in prison.'' I wanted to add, but that doesn't resign me to what happened to him. I did not say it, though. Mr. Gainsworth was trying to give me what comfort he could, and I must not throw it back in his face.

After dinner we went out onto a flag-stoned terrace for coffee and tiny glasses of Amaretto. The night was cool enough to made me glad I'd brought a shawl with me. It was pleasant, sitting out there in darkness relieved only by a first-quarter moon and the light from the dining room.

Perhaps in hope of coaxing his shy daughter into speech, Lawrence Gainsworth turned the talk back to New Mexico—its wildlife ranging from antelopes to prairie dogs, and its weather from frequent blizzards in the north to almost chronic drought here in the south. "But there are times when rain falls for so long that the dams spill over and sometimes break."

"I know," I said. "My mother's parents were drowned when water from a broken dam flooded down an arroyo."

"I remember that. It happened about forty-five years ago. Quite a few people besides your grandparents were drowned. And for about ten years after that everyone was nervous about the dams back here in the hills. During even moderate rainfall, the radio station in Bolton—that's the county seat—would broadcast an advisory to stay out of the arroyos. Do you remember that, Rachel?"

"I'm not sure, Father."

"Well, maybe you don't. You were quite young in those days. Now shall we look at your paintings?"

"Maybe Deborah wouldn't be interested, Father."

I said, not entirely sincere, "I'd love to see your work!"

We went back through the dining room. Johnny Whitecloud, still in jeans but with a white mess jacket covering his shirt, was helping Consuelo clear the table. He looked at me, but if he recognized me, his stolid face did not betray it. Briefly I wondered if I should tell Mr. Gainsworth about Johnny looking in that window at me. No, I decided. I did not want this kindly man to think that I was trying to place the label of Peeping Tom on this middle-aged man-child he had sheltered for so many years. Besides, Ben Farrel probably had been right in saying that the Indian was entirely harmless.

The Gainsworths and I went out into the hall and, at its end, climbed a flight of stairs. We passed two closed doors. He opened a third, reached inside, touched a light switch.

I found myself in a painter's studio, with

a big canvas, covered by a sheet, standing on an easel, and a solid wall of glass dimly mirroring the three of us as we stood there in the glow of overhead fluorescent lights. Then I turned my attention to the paintings on the walls.

They surprised me so that I actually felt embarrassed. Here were none of the amateurish daubs—inane still lifes and postcard-literal landscapes—that I had expected. (True, maybe I shouldn't have expected them, since Lawrence Gainsworth, a man of cultivated taste, had praised his daughter's work. But if romantic love is blind, parental love is often doubly so.)

The first painting I looked at was a still life, but it didn't show a vase of wild poppies or a glass jar holding dried weeds. It was a prickly pear cactus, its thick green segment looking as sensual as flesh, its flowers a bold scarlet. And although the next was a desert landscape, it could not have been entitled "Wild Flowers in the Spring." It showed the harsh desert floor and, in the distance, mesas that seemed to float, like those I'd seen earlier that day as I drove to and from the prison.

I'm far from an art expert. But like most New Yorkers I've window-shopped the galleries along Fifty-seventh Street and along Madison Avenue, and sometimes have even gone inside. It seemed to me that these paintings might be selected by such galleries.

I said, "Why, Rachel! These are—" Unable to come up with an adequate phrase, I said feebly, "I think they are excellent."

She blushed, actually blushed. "That's nice to hear."

I began to move slowly along the wall, looking at her work. She moved along with me, seeming to gain confidence every moment, her eyes bright now, her voice animated as she answered my comments and questions about each painting. She had a remarkable range, I soon realized. Some of her work, like the one of an old Conestoga wagon half buried by desert sand, was representational. Other paintings, like that prickly pear cactus, were surrealistic. Some, like the mesa painting, were a blend of the representational and abstract. Some were entirely abstract, like the one that showed a number of shapes— brown rectangles and red arrows and yellow spirals—against a stark white background. There was even a portrait, that of a man whom I recognized as a younger version of her father, seated at a piano.

As she talked of her work, I no longer pitied her. Just as her father had found freedom and an end to isolation in his reading, she had found it in her art.

I asked, "Where did you go to art school?"

"I didn't."

"What! You can't mean you are self-taught."

"Scarcely." Her father was smiling. "An instructor from the Wiley Institute of Art in New York spent four summers with us."

And not, I was sure, for just room and board. As I had learned from observing my stepfather, rich men were Mohammeds who summoned mountains at their convenience.

I said to Rachel, "Surely your pictures have been shown."

"Yes. First in Taos and later in San Francisco and New York. And quite a few have sold, either to private collectors or to institutions. The University of New Mexico owns three of mine."

Almost complacent now, so different from the woman who had sat silent and withdrawn, coffee cup in hand, on the dimly lighted terrace.

I said, "Oh, I like this one!"

The feathery brushwork was the sort I had become familiar with as I circled the room, but the subject matter—a tiny fawn lying by a woodland pool—was different from any of the others. The fawn and the green pines and the shadowed pool had a look of fantasy, as if they were part of a very superior illustration for a children's book.

"You do? I don't." She was frowning at the picture. "I think it's sentimental mush." She reached up, unhooked the picture from its holder. Bending, she turned it around and placed it, leaning, against the wall.

"Rachel!" I could tell by Lawrence Gainsworth's flush that he was both annoyed and embarrassed. Then he said to me, with a light laugh, "Artists can sometimes be rougher on their work than any critic, can't they?" He turned to his daughter. "But even if it is your painting," he said in that same light voice, "it's scarcely courteous to dispute your guest's opinion of it, now is it?"

Not speaking, she looked back at him. As the seconds lengthened I had a sense of some silent struggle going on between them.

The fact that I liked them both so much heightened my dismayed embarrassment. But then, no matter how nice a married couple seemed, or a parent and child, and no matter how well adjusted to each other, there could still be these sudden hostile flare-ups, for reasons unknowable to an outsider.

"Rachel, don't be difficult. If Deborah likes that painting, she might also like another one you did last week, the one of the little boy and the piebald pony."

"I can't show it to her."

"Why on earth not?."

"I painted it out and started another picture on top of it."

"Painted it out!"

"Yes. I decided it was even sillier than this one."

After a long moment her father said, "Rachel, you must be overtired."

I made a swift, awkward try at helping the situation. "And no wonder!" I said, glancing in feigned horror at my watch. "It's almost ten-thirty. I really must go, Mr. Gainsworth. I've had a very long day."

"Well, if you really must—" His regretful tone covered the relief I knew he must feel. "I'll bring the car around and drive you home. You can wait on the porch if you like."

He left us. Rachel accompanied me down the stairs and out onto the semicircular stone porch. Her manner was pleasant and friendly now, just as it had been in her studio until those last few moments. Perhaps she had felt no hostility toward me, but only to her father, for some reason I couldn't even guess at.

She said, "How long are you going to be out here, Deborah?"

Until I get him out of that place, I thought, or see there is no use in trying to. Aloud I said, "For another week, at least."

"Would you come back and see me in the daytime? I could show you my favorite place, up near the crest of the highest of these hills. From there you can see for miles. I'll ask Consuelo to pack a lunch for us. And I could set up my easel, if we decide to spend the rest of the day up there."

"That sounds great. I'd love to watch you work."

"Next Thursday my father is going up to Gallup for the day. He often goes there on business. That would be a good time.

Anyway, I'll call you at the hotel that morning."

The dark sedan, with her father behind the wheel, came around the corner of the house just then. He got out. I said good night to Rachel and walked down the steps to the car.

We drove in silence for only a few seconds. Then Lawrence Gainsworth said, "I'm sorry about that—that bit of unpleasantness back there. Rachel sometimes takes a dislike to some of her own work. I try to attribute it to artistic temperament, but just the same I find it exasperating."

I said, trying to be tactful, "Perhaps it's really rather admirable, a form of perfectionism, I mean."

That seemed to please him. "Perhaps. And then, she's a highly strung girl." He glanced at me, smiling. "I suppose you think that sounds absurd. To you Rachel must seem definitely middle-aged. But I still think of her as a girl."

I said, still striving for tactfulness, "Perhaps that's partly because she's so very attractive."

"Attractive, yes. But frail. And until she was four and a half she was such a sturdy child."

"She fell ill then?"

"Not exactly." For a few moments he looked straight ahead at the path the headlights cut through the darkness between walls of pines. Then he said, "It was my fault. My excuse is that Rachel's mother had died six months before, and I hadn't been able to adjust to life without her. I felt that I had to get away and travel for a while. I couldn't take Rachel with me, a child that young. And so I hired a nursemaid, a Scotswoman who had lived in San Francisco for several years, and who came highly recommended by friends of friends. I left Rachel in the woman's complete charge. I also asked her to look out for Johnny Whitecloud, a little Indian boy whose mother had died while in my employ.

"I traveled for six months," he went on. "England and then Italy and then Greece. When I got back I found that Rachel was thinner and quieter, but that didn't disturb me too much. I knew that growing children can change rapidly in appearance and temperament. I paid off the Scotswoman. She went back to San Francisco, and I again put Rachel in the charge of the young Navajo woman who had cared for her while her mother was alive."

He fell silent. The rapidly descending road now ran through thin stands of cedar. Finally he went on, "It took me several weeks to realize that something was seriously wrong. Again and again Rachel would awake screaming from nightmares. She was afraid of the dark—something new for her—and there was a room on the second floor, a sewing room, that seemed to terrify her so much that she refused to walk past it."

He paused. I asked, "Couldn't she explain what was wrong?"

"She either couldn't or wouldn't. And the two Guatemalan servants then in my employ, a cook and a housemaid, seemed struck dumb when I tried to question them about what had gone on in my absence. You see, the Scotswoman had told them that if they talked she would have them sent back to Guatemala. She couldn't have. Their papers were in order. Otherwise I would never have hired them. But that was what she threatened to do if they told me."

Again he paused. I said, somehow reluctant to know the answer, "Told you what?"

"About the Scotswoman's sadistic treatment of the children. I won't tell you all of it. You wouldn't want to hear it, and of course I still find it painful to talk about. But, anyway, the two Guatemalan servants finally broke down and told me that the Scotswoman had locked each of the children in the cellar at various times. Once she had left Johnny Whitecloud down there for two days without food or water. As for that sewing room on the second floor—"

He broke off, and then said rapidly, "No wonder it frightened Rachel so. To her it was an execution chamber. As punishment for something or other, the woman had threatened to hang her from the room's light fixture. She'd even placed the child on the sewing machine and tied a cord around her neck. Then she told Rachel that if she misbehaved again she really would hang her. And if Rachel ever talked about her, the woman said, she would come back and carry out the sentence."

I asked, feeling sick, "What did you do about the Scotswoman?"

"Nothing. My lawyer had a San Francisco associate go to the address the woman had given, but she'd left there weeks before, leaving no forwarding address. I did not try to find her, because by that time I had my hands full with Rachel. I took her several times to a child psychiatrist in El Paso, and for a while after that she seemed much better. But in her teens she again became emotionally unstable —shy and withdrawn much of the time, and sometimes flaring into anger. I took her out of the boarding school she'd been attending and hired a tutor for her."

"I suppose you again took her to a psychiatrist?"

"Several of them. The consensus seemed to be that the worst thing would be to try to force her out of her reclusiveness, force her to go to college, for instance. So I've allowed her to live as she wants to live."

I thought of her in her studio, cheeks flushed with pleasure at my praise, voice animated as she described how and why she had chosen to paint each of her canvases. "It seems to have worked out fairly well."

"Yes. Naturally I would have liked for her to marry. But she seems happy in her work and her surroundings. And I'm selfish enough to be glad that I still have her companionship."

We were on the desert floor now, driving along the almost empty county road toward Prosperity. He said, "Forgive me for talking so much about my personal problems. But I knew Rachel must have struck you as strange, and I wanted you to understand.''

Why had he cared whether or not I understood? Was it because he had taken a liking to me? Or was it just that Lawrence Gainsworth, almost as reclusive as his daughter, could not resist discussing her with others when he had the opportunity?

"Now about you, Deborah. How long do you intend to stay here?"

For a while tonight, good food and good talk had made me forget that so far I had learned nothing, nothing at all, that might help me free my father. But now I again felt weighted with a sense of futility

"I don't know," I said. "I want to talk to the mother of that—that little girl who was killed. I'll do that tomorrow morning. And afterward I'd like to visit that arroyo where my grandparents were staying when that flood hit. Outside of that, all I can think of to do is to stay here in town, at least until the next visiting day at the prison. I'll keep asking questions of everyone, keep hoping that I will learn something that will help—''

"I'm afraid you won't enjoy your visit to

the McCabe house."

"So people keep telling me."

"And with reason. Loretta McCabe is an alcoholic, and so is her paramour." From his tone I could tell he liked using the archaic term. "And Loretta's mother, who lives with them, is a profane old harridan."

"Nevertheless, I think that if anyone might have an idea as to who really killed her little girl, it would be Daisy's mother. Oh, maybe she doesn't have any conscious idea, but perhaps if I jog her memory—"

My voice trailed off. After a moment Mr. Gainsworth said, "My dear, I sympathize with what you're doing, and I wish you the best of fortune. But please do be careful, and not only for your own sake. Think how utterly it would devastate your father to learn that you had come to any sort of harm through trying to help him."

"I'll be careful," I said, although just how I was to do so I didn't know.

Again we drove for a while in silence. Then I said, "May I ask you a question?"

"Fire away."

"Why is it that you've befriended my father all these years?"

"I don't understand. Why shouldn't we be friends?"

140

I decided to be blunt. "You're rich. He's been poor all his life. You're well educated. He isn't, at least not formally."

Mr. Gainsworth nodded. "That's true. If it weren't for what happened to him, I suppose I'd have gone on having the same friendly but reserved relationship I have with many craftsmen and tradesmen around here. But when he was arrested I couldn't believe he was guilty. At first it was just a matter of sympathy for him and your mother. But over the years, through our correspondence, we've become real friends."

Moments later he stopped the car in front of the hotel. I said, "I've enjoyed this evening very much." And I had. Except for my brief embarrassment when Rachel and her father had clashed, I'd found the evening pleasant indeed.

"I'm very glad you could have dinner with us. I could tell how much my daughter, too, enjoyed having you there."

He walked with me into the lobby, where we exchanged good-nights. He went out then, and I started toward the stairs.

The elderly night clerk called, "Oh, Miss Channing." I turned. "A gentleman telephoned you twice this evening."

My heart leapt. "Who was he?"

"He didn't leave his name. He just said he'd call again in half an hour." He turned to look at the old-fashioned round wooden clock affixed to the wall behind him. Its hands pointed to three of eleven. "He should be calling again any minute now."

Chief Ben Farrel? No, he would have left his name, and even if he didn't, the desk clerk would have recognized his voice. And so in all probability it had been Greg, calling from New York. True, it was two in the morning back there, but that wouldn't stop Greg, not if he felt he needed to talk to me.

"Thank you," I said, and hurried up the stairs to my room.

CHAPTER
TWELVE

I HAD JUST hung my shawl in the closet when the telephone rang. Swiftly I lifted the phone from its cradle and said hello.

Greg said, "Deborah?" There was a flatness in his voice that made my heart contract with premonitory fear.

"Yes, Greg."

"How are you?"

"I'm fine," I said automatically. "And you?"

"All right."

He was silent for so long after that that I said, "You still there?"

"Yes. I was wondering if you'd found out anything to—to help your father."

And to help him, Gregory Vanlieden. Help him to reconcile his parents to the idea of bringing Joe Hartley's daughter into the family.

I said, in a voice as flat as his own, "No, nothing."

Again there was silence for several seconds. Then he said, "I'm flying out there tomorrow. The airline tells me the nearest airport to you is at Silver City, so I'll rent a car there. I should reach you by late afternoon."

"Why?"

"I don't know what you mean."

"Why are you flying out here?"

I waited, hoping against hope that he would say, "I miss you so much that I can't bear for us to be apart any longer."

Instead he said, "I have to talk to you."

I managed to say, "Can't you talk about it over the phone?"

"It wouldn't be right to do that."

Men like Greg had a code. There was a wrong way and a right way, a cowardly way and a decent way to do everything, even breaking off with a girl. You did it in person, not over the phone.

I said, "Then I'll say it for you. You don't feel you can marry the daughter of a man who has spent twenty years in prison. You wouldn't really want to even if it

144

turned out that he'd been wrongly convicted, because the taint would still be there."

"Deborah, there's my family, my friends." His voice was wretchedly ashamed. "It's not that I didn't love you. I still love you. But—"

"You don't have to justify yourself. When you asked me to marry you, you didn't know I was a convict's daughter. I have no right to try to hold you to anything. As I told you in New York, such a marriage wouldn't be good enough for either of us. I said we should both think things over, and it's obvious that you've done just that."

Several seconds passed before he said, "Deborah, please believe that it will take a long, long time for me to get over this. I mean—"

"I know what you mean. You want me to know that you haven't come to your decision lightly. I realize that."

"If there was something more I could say—"

"There isn't. Good-bye, Greg."

I hung up. At the moment I felt numb, but I knew that wouldn't last. Soon the pain would begin to tear at me.

I walked over to the window and looked down. Across the street no one moved along the sidewalk. The bar's neon sign had been turned off for the night. Only a green-shaded street lamp illuminated the harshly plain brick buildings and the empty pavement. For the first time I realized that the view from this window was like an Edward Hopper painting of a street in a lonely small town, a place so bleak that you felt that any love that might manage to bloom here was doomed to early withering.

CHAPTER
THIRTEEN

I DID NOT fall asleep until after I heard an early riser stirring about in the room above my own. It seemed to me that only minutes later my traveling alarm clock's ring brought me back to consciousness.

Around three o'clock of that grim night I had gotten up and set the alarm for eight. I would call Barry Greenwood in New York, I had resolved, and ask if he had found buyers for either the duplex or the Georgica Pond house. Rather than keep floundering in a sea of pain, I would start planning realistically for the rest of my life. The lawyer, in semiretirement for the past few years, often took afternoons off, so it would be best to call him before noon, New York time.

When he came on the line we exchanged how-are-yous. My response was a mechanical "Fine, thank you." Then I said, "I've been wondering what my financial situation is."

"I was about to call you on that. I signed a binder yesterday for the duplex. The price is not what I hoped, but on the other hand the buyers are willing to delay taking possession for two months after the deal's completed. Thus you'll have time to dispose of the rest of the things you want to get rid of and time to find a place to live."

"I'll need those two months. What about the Georgica Pond house?"

"The market in the Hamptons is softer than I had realized. But I have several offers and should be able to dispose of it before the next payment on that whopping mortgage is due."

He was silent for a moment and then said, "I'm sorry to tell you this, but your situation isn't good. I'd hoped you could salvage enough to buy yourself a small apartment. But it looks as if you'll clear about twenty thousand, or maybe a little more."

"Well, that's better than nothing."

"Have you heard anything that might

help your father?''

''Not yet. But I've seen him. He's grateful to you for handling the correspondence between him and my mother all those years.''

''Will you see him again?''

''Yes, next visiting day.''

''Well, give him my best.'' Again he paused, and then asked, ''When are you coming back, Debby?''

''I don't know. My leave was for only two weeks, but I suppose they would give me more time if I asked for it.''

''I'm sure they would,'' he said swiftly, as if glad of the chance to say something optimistic. ''Your firm thinks highly of you.''

We talked for perhaps a minute longer, and then hung up. Almost immediately I realized that he hadn't asked about Greg. Surely that must mean that Barry Greenwood knew that Greg was no longer a part of my life. Not that he could have known about that telephone conversation the night before. It must be just that the lawyer, a realist, knew that when all is said and done the Vanliedens of the world don't marry convicts' daughters.

I put on a shirtwaist dress of blue denim

and went down to the luncheonette for breakfast. When I'd given my order for orange Danish to the red-haired waitress, Nancy, I asked, "Do you know where Loretta McCabe lives?"

"Sure." Her reddish-brown eyes were bright with interest. Like everyone else in town, she must have known by this time who I was and why I was here. "She lives just east of town. You know where the post office is, at the very end of Main Street?"

I nodded.

"Well, she's the fourth or fifth house beyond that, on the south side of the highway. A little green stucco. You can't miss it."

"Thank you." I looked around the room. "Do you have a pay phone?"

"No pay phone. And if you're thinking of calling Loretta, it wouldn't do you any good. They don't have a phone."

She lingered a moment, as if hoping for more conversation, and then went to get my order. I would go to see Loretta McCabe immediately, I decided, and not just because I needed distraction from thoughts of Greg. It was also because I was more determined than ever to free my father. That might seem odd, considering that part of my motivation in coming to New Mexico had been the desire to remove obstacles to my marriage. But now that Greg and I had broken off with each other, my father was all that I had left in this world. Out of the shambles my life had become of late, I was determined to pluck one prize, my father's freedom.

I had no trouble in finding the house, a green stucco bungalow from which the plaster had peeled in leprous spots, revealing the lathes underneath. I did have trouble in parking. A ditch had been dug in front of the McCabe house as well as those on either side of it. Perhaps the county was laying a new sewer pipe. Anyway, there were red flags and "men at work" signs, although no men were visible at the moment. I stopped in the road for a few seconds. Then I drove over two wide planks which, spanning the ditch, joined the highway to the McCabe driveway. I stopped the car. Ahead of me, through the open door of a garage, I could see an old blue pickup truck.

By the time I walked around the corner of the house to the tiny square of cement porch, a woman had opened the door and pushed the screen back. I gained a swift impression of overweight, of red hair, brown-gray at the roots, and of a knee-length blue chemise of some synthetic material, liberally spotted with stains. Although the day was cool, she wore no stockings. There were a few bruises on her thick white legs.

I said, "Mrs. McCabe?"

"That's right. And you don't have to tell me who you are. Joe Hartley's daughter. I been expecting you."

She sounded almost friendly, as if she'd found the expectation pleasant. Perhaps she had. Perhaps any novelty was welcome, even a visit from the daughter of a man who, twenty years earlier, had been sent to prison for killing her child.

"Come in," she said.

Everything in the room, from the TV set to the sagging blue velour sofa to the tan rug, was either stained or burn-marked or nicked or, in the case of the TV set, all three. On the mantel above the fake fireplace, even a new-looking plastic nymph, seminude and with a clock set in her stomach, had a missing nose. At the windows, flowered draperies of some sort of plastic flanked curtains with sagging hems.

152

"Take the load off," she said, waving me to a blue velour armchair. I sat in it. Its springless seat sank so alarmingly that for a moment I thought I was going to land on the floor. She herself sat down on the matching sofa. A half-filled glass and a bottle labeled "Old Corporal Rye" stood before her on a blond coffee table scarred with cigarette burns.

"Felt a cold coming on this morning," she explained. "You join me?"

"Thanks, but it's a little early for me."

"Well, if you don't mind," she said, and took a swallow of her drink.

I said, "I guess you know why I'm here."

"Sure. You got some idea you can get your dad out of prison. Well, I sympathize with you, honey. Honest to God I do, even though it was my own kid your old man—I mean, it wasn't your fault he did that, was it?"

Looking at her bloated face, I thought with sudden irrelevance that this woman must be about the same age my exquisitely groomed and still lovely mother had been. I said, "But he didn't do it."

"Yes, I know that's what you've been saying. But look, kid. Look at the evidence. I mean, starting out with the fact that my little girl had been seen riding in your father's truck several times—"

I said, to stop her, "Yes, I know the evidence." I couldn't bear another recital of where Daisy's body had been found, and of the nugget in her hand, and the rest of it. "But can't you remember anything that might indicate that someone else—"

"No, I can't." She took another swallow of her drink. "All the evidence fitted Joe Hartley like a glove. You'd better face it. It was Joe Hartley who killed my little girl—"

Her mouth trembled. It was the first sign of emotional disturbance she had shown. I said, "Please, please forgive me for distressing you like this. But my father staying in prison won't bring your little girl back. So please, please, if you can think of anything—I mean, can you tell me just what she said about this man she called Joe?"

She had turned sullen. "I didn't pay much attention to her. I had other things on my mind."

I wondered what things. "But you did remember that she talked of someone named Joe."

"Yes! But I didn't remember it until after they found my baby in Joe

Hartley's backyard!"

Afraid that she might become angry enough to order me out of her house, I said placatingly, "Mrs. McCabe, forgive me! I know how hard it must be for you to—to probe your memory about this. But didn't she know anyone else named Joe?"

"Sure. Only a damn fool would think she didn't." Her tone was definitely combative now. "World's full of Joes. I think there was even a couple of Joes in her class at school. But there was only one Joe in town who could have done it."

"But there must have been—"

"No must about it! And anyway, maybe the Joe she was talking about wasn't even real."

"Not real!"

"You heard me. If you was a mother you'd know kids are like that. They make up things. When Daisy was five she kept talking about May and I thought May was some kid in her kindergarten class and then one day she told me May had got her tail caught under a gate, and then it came out. May was a make-believe squirrel. For all I know Joe was a make-believe horse or a prairie dog or some damn thing."

Until that dismaying moment, I hadn't

realized how much I had counted on the reality of that other Joe, the one who might have been responsible for Daisy's death.

"But I really don't think she was talking about some horse or prairie dog. She was talking about Joe Hartley!" Her face twisted. "My baby!" Her voice rose. "That dirty bastard took my baby and—"

A door across the room burst open. A nearly bald man of about fifty stood there, wearing a sleeveless undershirt and a pair of khaki pants belted around his ample waist.

"Can't a man get any sleep in his own house?"

She turned a tearful face toward him. "I got a right to cry if I want!" Then with an attempt at formality, she turned back to me. "This is my friend, Ed Smith. Ed, this is—"

"I know who she is. And I know you're drunk. Not even ten in the morning, and you're stinking."

"Look who's talking! Only reason you're not drinking is you been asleep."

"That's a lie!"

In succinct Anglo-Saxon, she told him what to do. He left the room, slamming the door behind him.

She turned toward me, her face accusatory. "See what you done? Didn't your old man do enough to us, without you coming out here, raking up stuff people want to forget, causing family quarrels—"

There was nothing to say except goodbye, and so I said it and walked to the door. She shouted something after me, but by then I had neared the corner of the house and could not distinguish the words.

I got in the Datsun, but before I could insert the ignition key I heard a tapping noise. I looked to my right. A woman stood at the window of what was apparently the kitchen, since a bottle of detergent stood on the sill. Her old face, framed in untidy white hair, wore an urgent expression. Once she had my attention, she placed a finger to her lips. After that, with fingers bunched together, her hand moved slowly right through the air. Then the moving fingers made a right turn and, after a few inches, stopped.

After a moment I got it. She wanted me to back out onto the street, drive until I reached the end of the ditch, and then stop at the roadside and wait for her. I nodded, put the car in gear, and backed carefully over the planks spanning the ditch. Seconds later I parked in front of another stucco house, a tan one considerably more spruce than the McCabes'.

I waited. Then in the rearview mirror I saw a thin youth of about sixteen approaching through the weeds on the other side of the ditch. He wore ragged jeans, with a khaki shirt hanging loose over his belt. His head was shaved in what was perhaps the latest style among local teenagers, with only a narrow strip of blondish hair running, Indian-brave fashion, from his forehead to the nape of his neck. His right arm cradled an air rifle. He gave me a long, curious stare and then went up the walk to the tan stucco house.

Its door had just closed behind him when, again looking in the rearview mirror, I saw the elderly woman emerge from the McCabe driveway and, with surprising speed, walk toward me through the weeds. I swung the door back and she got in beside me.

"I'm Loretta's mother."

Her wrinkled features showed a certain refinement. I could tell that she'd been attractive once, far more so than her daughter. That was why her next words came as a bit of a shock.

"Look, girlie. I can tell you the son of a

158

bitch who done it."

As I stared at her, speechless, with mingled disbelief and hope, she went on, "I heard you was in town and trying to get Joe Hartley off the hook, so I sneaked this out of Ed's dresser drawer. I been carrying it around for days."

She plunged her hand into the pocket of her rumpled print dress and brought out a worn manila envelope. She took it and unfolded the document inside. It said that on a date twenty-nine years earlier Edward Joseph Smith had been honorably discharged from the armed forces of the United States.

"You see that?" she said excitedly. Her gnarled forefinger, liberally rimmed with black, pointed out the middle name. "There's your Joe!"

I said, after a moment's bitter disappointment, "I'm afraid, Mrs.—"

"Carruthers. Elsie Carruthers."

"I'm afraid, Mrs. Carruthers, that this isn't sufficient evidence—"

"Evidence? Then I'll give you evidence. Ed Smith hated Daisy. He was always yelling at her. And it wasn't just me that suspected Ed. Loretta did too."

"Mrs. Carruthers, that can't be. If she'd

suspected him she would have told the police."

"You think that because you don't know my daughter! She was crazy about Ed. Still is, for that matter. Just the same, she might of turned him in if she hadn't been drinking so hard. Person drinks that hard, their brains turn to mush, and they can't carry through anything from one day to the next.

"Loretta always was a damn fool," she went on broodingly. "I guess you wonder why she and Ed ain't married."

It hadn't occurred to me to wonder. I made a noncommittal sound.

"Loretta wanted to marry him. That was why she got a divorce, two years after McCabe—Russel McCabe was her husband's name—walked out on her. But Ed kept stalling, and finally it turned out he already had a wife back in Dallas. She's Catholic and won't give him a divorce, and he's afraid of going to jail for bigamy."

"Oh, so that's it." Then: "Mrs. Carruthers, if you suspected Ed Smith, why didn't you tell the authorities?"

"And maybe have him and Loretta throw me out on my you-know-what? No thanks!" The lined face turned anxious. "You won't tell them that I'm the one who put you on the right track, will you? Don't say nothing about my showing you that discharge.''

"No, I won't." I put the document back in its envelope and handed it to her. "Better return that to his bureau as soon as you can."

She stuffed the envelope into her pocket. "Just leave me out of it. Just you go ahead and gather as much evidence as you need. Maybe you could hire some detectives to nail him. I hear you're a rich girl, on account of your mother married rich. You ought to be able to get yourself some real smart detectives."

Rich girl. "Maybe I'll do that. But hadn't you better go back now, before they miss you?"

"You're right. Good luck, girlie. And don't ever tell nobody we had this little chat."

She started to get out of the car. I said, "One thing more, Mrs. Carruthers. Can you think of any reason why Ed Smith or anyone else would have—have buried that child in my father's backyard?"

"You bet your you-know-what I can! Ed Smith hated Joe Hartley, maybe even more than he hated Daisy. Joe found out Ed had stolen a spare tire off his truck, and he came here to get it, and the two of them got into a fight. Your pa thrashed Ed within an inch of his life. Then he went in the garage and got his tire and took it home. Ed hated him from then on.''

''I see. Well, thank you, Mrs. Carruthers.''

In the rearview mirror I watched her progress through the weeds to the McCabe driveway. Then I just sat there, reflecting that my visit to Loretta McCabe had been worse than futile. Oh, I had learned that Ed Smith's middle name was Joe, and that he'd disliked Daisy, and had a fistfight with my father, but that scarcely added up to proof that he was the one who belonged behind those prison gates.

What had been most dismaying about my visit was the discovery that Daisy had been the sort of child who had imaginary friends. I had been so sure he existed, that other Joe, and so hopeful that learning his identity might lead to my father's freedom. And now to discover that perhaps ''Joe'' had been a phantom of a lonely child's imagination—perhaps not even an imaginary human being, but some kind of animal.

I became conscious that the bright sun-light hurt my eyes. Undoubtedly that was because I had lain sleepless nearly all night, thinking of Greg.

But I was not going to start thinking about him now. Instead I would keep moving. That arroyo where my grand-parents' camper had stood, for instance. I could go there now.

I switched on the ignition, made a U-turn, and drove back toward Main Street.

CHAPTER
FOURTEEN

THE DATSUN'S FUEL gauge showed that the tank was almost empty. That was not surprising. I had not bought any gas since I rented the car in Silver City. I passed the bank and then turned into the Jay-Bee Service Station.

A man dressed in a white coverall, with "Jay-Bee" stitched in red on the breast pocket, came out of the glass-enclosed office. Pleasant-faced and with straight gray-blond hair, he appeared to be about fifty, although his lean figure suggested a younger man. He smiled and asked, "Fill 'er up?"

"Yes, please."

I sat there for a few minutes, vaguely aware of the ping-ping-ping of the gas pump. He racked the hose, took my twenty-dollar bill into the station house, returned with my change. He said, somewhat hesitantly, "You're Joe Hartley's daughter, aren't you?"

I nodded.

"I hear you went up to the—I hear you went up to see him."

No wonder Prosperity didn't have a newspaper, even a weekly. It didn't need one.

"Yes, I did."

"If you go again, will you tell him Jay Barnwell sends his regards?"

"I will. You're Mr. Barnwell?"

"Yes. That's why we named the station Jay-Bee. Jay for me and Bee for my wife, Beatrice. Her folks put up half the money for the station. Anyway, your daddy and I used to be good friends. Went hunting together a lot."

He hesitated and then said in an embarrassed tone, "If you get a chance, tell him I'm sorry I haven't gone to visit him or even written to him in all these years."

I said, with a certain coolness, "Do you want me to give him a reason?"

Again he hesitated. "Well, I'm sure Joe knows the reason. It's Bee." Even though there was no woman in sight except myself, he glanced nervously over his shoulder. "She'd always liked him a lot. But after —after what happened, she couldn't stand the thought of either of us having anything to do with him."

I said, still with that coolness, "And how did you feel about him?"

"Hell, I never thought Joe Hartley killed that kid. I knew that things looked bad for him, just as bad as they possibly could without an eyewitness, but just the same I'll never believe he did it."

My heart warmed to him, just as it had toward Lawrence Gainsworth when he expressed his belief in my father's innocence. At least two people in this town believed him incapable of killing anyone. True, a third person, Elsie Carruthers, had told me she thought he was innocent. But she really didn't count, since her obvious intent was not to see justice done, but to get her daughter's boyfriend in as much trouble as possible.

"I'll tell him, Mr. Barnwell. I'm sure he'll be glad to hear from you, even indirectly. Good-bye for now."

I had left the station and driven perhaps a hundred yards before I realized I should have asked him where the arroyo was located, the one in which my grandparents had drowned. Well, no matter. I could stop at the police station and ask Ben Farrel. True, that wall of water had raced down from the broken dam forty-five years ago, long before Ben was born. But that flood must be part of the town's folklore. Probably he could tell me the exact spot where my grandparents' camper had stood.

I parked the Datsun in front of Town Hall. The gray-haired woman in the police station's outer office said, "You looking for Ben?"

I nodded.

"Well, he's gone over to Bolton, the county seat. The police there are holding a man for sticking up a restaurant. They think he may be the same man who held up the luncheonette here in town a couple of months ago. Anyway Ben and an eyewitness have gone over to try to identify him, and they took Hal Newby with them." I must have given her an inquiring look, because she explained: "Hal's Ben's deputy on the day shift. Cliff Sorenson takes over at night. My name, by the way, is Dot Canby."

"How do you do?" I said, smiling, and

then asked, "Do you have any idea when Mr. Farrel will be back?"

"No. But could I help you?"

"I imagine so. It's about my grand-parents' death about forty-five years ago. They were caught in this flood—

"Yes, I know."

Was there anything about me these people didn't know? "I'd like to drive out to where it happened."

"There I can't help you much. I never learned to drive—silly, but there it is—and I've got no sense of direction. All I'm sure of is that it's near that religious colony."

"Then I guess I'd better drive out there and ask them."

"That would be the surest way of finding the right spot." Something in her expression made me think that she already knew the details of my first visit to Beersheba.

I drove the rest of the way through town, continued along the level highway, turned right at the sign pointing toward Beersheba. I was not at all sure why I was seeking out the spot where that young couple had died nearly a half century ago. Perhaps it was some vague sense of filial duty to those forebears I'd never known. Perhaps it was an even vaguer hope that by going there I might—somehow, some way—learn more about a second tragic event that, twenty-odd years later, had imprisoned my father and sent my mother fleeing with me across the continent.

Only one thing I could be sure of. I had hoped that by keeping in motion I could outdistance the anguish of that phone call from Greg.

But suddenly it wasn't working. The memory of Greg's face, his voice, his touch overwhelmed me. I wanted to turn off onto the sandy earth and stop the car and then double up over the wheel, as if from some actual physical pain.

Instead, still driving, I tried to force my thoughts away from lost love. Think about your talk with Barry Greenwood, I ordered myself. Think of the twenty thousand or so he says you'll be able to salvage from the wreckage. How should you invest it? A CD? Treasury notes? A flyer in the stock market?

Well, in one way I was lucky. As an employee of an investment firm, I would not lack for advisors.

The windbreak of junipers loomed up ahead. Beyond it straw-hatted men and sunbonneted women still worked between the neat rows of green, growing things. Today their inspection of me as I passed was not cursory. Several of them leaned on their hoes and stared. Even from a distance I could read the disapproval in their attitudes. So this time they knew who I was. Daughter of that errant Sara Campbell who had not waited for the elders to choose a husband for her. Daughter, too, of a man convicted of a terrible crime. I told myself that their resentment of my reappearance was understandable. After all, my mother had owed her very life to them.

I entered Beersheba's wide main street. Here, too, there was something different today. In front of the store from which the colonists sold their products to tourists stood an elderly Cadillac with an Ohio license plate. I parked in front of it, got out, and entered the store.

Two middle-aged women were exclaiming over the patchwork quilts, hung on one wall. Their husbands, looking bored, stood by with hands in their pockets. Mrs. Jenkins again sat behind the counter. Despite the alarm that leaped into her face at sight of me, her fingers kept on knitting. Through the archway I could see Samuel Jenkins glaring at me from above that John Brown beard.

Mrs. Jenkins rose, laid her knitting on the counter, and hurried toward me. I said quickly, "I just came for some information, Mrs. Jenkins."

"Let's go outside."

She did not seize my elbow and propel me through the doorway, but the effect was much the same. She said, "Why have you come back here? Don't you realize that you upset my husband?"

"I'm sorry." I meant it. I was sure she found even an un-upset Samuel Jenkins hard to live with.

I looked down the street toward the open door of the furniture shop. Was my mother's ex-suitor watching us? I had no way of knowing.

"I'm sorry," I repeated, "and I'll stay only a minute. I just wanted to ask the location of that arroyo in which my grandparents drowned. Can you tell me?"

"Of course I can!" She went on rapidly, "Drive back toward the highway. About half a mile beyond the windbreak you'll see a road leading off to the right. It's little more than a track, so you'll have to keep a sharp lookout for it. Follow it until you get to the arroyo. There used to be a bridge there, but it's been gone for years and years."

"Is that the spot where my grandparents—"

"No, not right there." She looked at the Datsun. "But since you're not using oversized tires you'd best leave your car there and then walk about a half mile to your left. You'll see that the arroyo's walls are a lot lower there, and more sloping. There was plenty of room to park a camper down there beside the little stream in the canyon's bottom. And another thing. There's also a big boulder down there, with some old Indian drawings on it. I mean really old, maybe a thousand years. The people from here who visited the Campbells a few days before the flood said that their camper was parked right beside the boulder."

"Thank you."

"You're welcome. Now please go. And for everybody's sake, don't come back."

CHAPTER
FIFTEEN

I RETRACED MY way past the men and women in the fields, who again paused in their work to stare at me. I was not to come back, Mrs. Jenkins had said, "for everybody's sake." She had not added, "including your own," but the implication had been clear. I didn't feel threatened, though. No matter how much they, in their self-righteousness, might thunder at me, I felt sure that men like Samuel Jenkins and Nathaniel Crisp would draw the line at physical violence.

After I'd passed the windbreak I began to drive slowly, glancing alternately at the roadside and the car's odometer. It was a good thing I did. Otherwise I might have missed the road, not much more than two tire tracks, which led off to the right.

I had traveled about three miles of its length when I glimpsed buildings up ahead. As I drew closer I saw that they were a little house and some sort of shed, obviously long deserted, and far more dilapidated than even the dwelling where I had spent the first three years of my life. The wooden building nearest the road, a one-room shack with a partially collapsed lean-to, had taken on the sheen of driftwood. The larger structure behind it, most of its roof missing, but with one half of its wide wooden door in place, looked equally old. Who, I wondered, had built this place? Someone who had hoped to raise a few chickens or even sheep? Some prospector who had searched for ore in the arroyos or in the hills to the west? Or had some eccentric of the type deserts attract chosen to live like a hermit in that lean-to, with perhaps a cow and a horse or mule stabled in the shed? In any case, it was obvious that decades ago those buildings had been given over to the sun and the wind and the small creatures of the desert.

I drove on. Perhaps five minutes later I saw that ahead of me the ground gave way. I stopped at the arroyo's edge. The small canyon narrowed here, which undoubtedly was why a bridge had been built at this point. All that remained of the bridge was one tall piling, which stood in the tiny stream at the canyon's bottom, and a few feet of jagged planking, which stuck out from the opposite wall. I wondered whether the bridge had been destroyed in some flood, such as the one that had killed my grandparents. Perhaps. Or perhaps it had been neglected until it just rotted away.

As Mrs. Jenkins had instructed, I got out of the car and walked to my left. Gradually the arroyo widened and the slope of its banks became gentle. Then I saw the jagged boulder. It stood about six feet high, with the narrow stream at the canyon's bottom parting to flow past it.

I descended the gentle slope, thinking as I did so of that camper, with my young grandfather at the wheel, driving down this same slope. Probably, for safety's sake, my grandmother had stood at the top of the bank, holding in her arms the infant who was to become my mother.

At the foot of the slope I stopped at the stream's edge and looked at the still bright pictures painted in some sort of red pigment on the boulder's fairly smooth surface.

There was a circle with rays streaming from its circumference. It looked much like the pictures with which children and some cartoonists depict the sun. There was a smaller circle, which I knew must be the moon. And there were stick figures of men and of animals that looked like deer.

Why had the Indians chosen this spot for their paintings, paintings that I knew must have magical significance? Because this place was beautiful? Perhaps. Anyway, it certainly was beautiful. Long wild grass grew underfoot. Partway up the gentle slope opposite me, a clump of desert willows leaned toward the little stream.

How pleased, I reflected, that young couple of forty-five years ago must have been with their camping spot. I could imagine my grandmother kneeling beside the stream, doing laundry that had accumulated during the long trip from the East. I could imagine how, even though they may have cooked their meals inside the camper, they must have eaten them on the blanket-spread grass, with small Sara lying on her back and kicking her sock-clad feet as she drank formula from a bottle.

But finally the rain started, perhaps gentle in the afternoon, but growing heavier after dark. Probably my grandfather, aware that the small stream widened, had moved the camper to a spot a few feet away from it. Then they must have gone to bed, glad that their only child was warm and dry in the infirmary at Beersheba. It probably never occurred to them that they themselves were in danger. Easterners, they did not know about the fury of Southwestern cloudbursts, or about that dam back in the hills.

I thought then of how, if it had not been for her cold, tiny Sara would have been in the camper that night when the deadly wall of water swept down the arroyo. And if she had been, then I would never have been born, never have grown up to be sitting here on this unclouded afternoon, eyes burning after an almost sleepless night, heart heavy, and yet still able to appreciate the loveliness of this unexpectedly verdant spot.

My thoughts shifted then to the odds against myself or any one individual being born—astronomical odds, I'd read somewhere. And I began to feel the baffled wonderment we all feel when we ask ourselves whether any event, including one's own birth, is the product of happenstance or some sort of design.

Gradually my thoughts blurred, until all I had was a vague awareness of my surroundings. The sun warm on my face and hands. The rippling sound of the stream. The harsh call of a bird—lighter in color than an eastern jay, but unmistakably jaylike in its shape and jeering voice—from the willow clump. I think I even slept a little, cheek resting on my updrawn knees, because I suddenly had a distinct sense that the sunlight fell at a different slant than it had moments ago.

The hands of my watch pointed to almost two-thirty. I stood up and took a last look around me. I was glad I had come here. It had made me feel very close, not only to that young couple I had never known, but to the infant my own mother once had been.

Turning, I climbed the bank's gentle slope. When I reached the Datsun I managed to back it, without getting stuck, onto the sandy earth bordering what had once been a road, but was now only two shallow ruts. Then I started back the way I had come.

Soon I could see ahead the little shanty and its barn, or storage house, or whatever it had been, dilapidated and yet beautiful with those satiny old boards gleaming in the sun. I thought of stopping to look inside the house. But no. I was very tired. Better to get back to the hotel and try to nap. I drove on past.

A cracking noise, followed by a whine so high-pitched that I could hear it above the sound of the car's small engine.

That first shot startled me so that my foot left the accelerator. The Datsun bucked and almost stalled. Another shot. This time I saw sand spurt up ahead of me and about five feet to my left.

My terrified gaze flew to the rearview mirror. Someone had poked a rifle through a window of the shanty. Sun glinted on its barrel.

I had the car under control now. I stepped hard on the accelerator. As the Datsun leapt foward I heard a final shot. Then silence, except for the engine's sound and the hammer of my own blood in my ears. Again I looked in the rearview mirror. No rifle in the shanty's window now.

With my stomach gathering into a knot, I thought, what if I had stopped? Stopped and gone in there and met the rifleman face to face?

Probably he had some sort of car hidden

in that old barn. What if he had chased and overtaken me out here in this waste? Again my eyes flew to the rearview mirror. No car. No sign of any movement whatsoever back there.

As my first terror subsided, I had a growing sense of excited discovery. Someone had tried to kill me. And why should he try to do that unless he was afraid of me, afraid that I would learn the truth about Daisy McCabe's death?

Surely this should be proof enough even for Ben Farrel that, despite the evidence his father had assembled, it was not Joe Hartley who should have gone to prison.

Who knew that I would be out here on this desert flat today? Mrs. Jenkins, of course. Within a minute or two after my departure, her husband must have extracted from her the reason for my visit, and soon after that the whole colony must have known. Earlier, at the police station, I had asked Dot Canby, the gray-haired clerk, for directions to the arroyo. I had no way of estimating how many people she had told— people who had dropped in at police headquarters, people in other Town Hall offices, perhaps people in the luncheonette if she had gone there at noon. Anyone in this whole area could have known, including Lawrence Gainsworth, hard as it was to imagine him shooting anyone from ambush. In fact, I had a vague recollection that I had told him I intended to visit the place where my grandparents' camper had stood.

Still no sign of any pursuer. I had reached the road leading to Beersheba now. I sped along in the opposite direction, toward the county highway. Once I had turned left toward Prosperity, only a trace of my former fear mingled with my sense of grim triumph.

I parked the car in front of the police station and went inside. Dot Canby, typing at a desk, looked up at me. "He's back. I guess it'll be all right if you want to go in."

"Thank you."

I knocked at the door of the inner office and called, "Mr. Farrel?"

"Come in, Miss Channing."

Surprised that he had recognized my voice, I opened the door and went in. He got up from his desk chair, took one look at me, and asked, "What the hell happened?"

"Somebody tried to kill me."

After a moment he said, voice heavy with skepticism, "Are you sure?" But for just an instant I had seen certain dismay in his eyes, as if the thought of someone trying to kill me had struck him as not entirely improbable.

"Of course I'm sure! Someone with a rifle fired three shots at me."

"Where did this happen?"

"About two miles from that arroyo where my grandparents—"

"Oh, yes. Dot told me you'd asked her how to get out there. Well, sit down. Tell me about it."

I did. He asked a few questions. How far past the shack was I when the first shot was fired? (About two hundred feet.) Did I catch even a glimpse of someone inside the shack? (No.) Did I see any sign of another car? (No.)

Finally he said, "Where's your car now?"

"Out front."

"Let's go take a look at it."

Out on the sidewalk he said, "It would be best if you drove around to the police parking lot. I don't want to attract any kibitzers."

I got in the Datsun and drove it onto the lot to the right of Town Hall. I parked it near what I suspected was Prosperity's entire fleet of police cars—two white Chevrolets with blue revolving roof lights.

By the time I got out of the Datsun, Ben Farrel had walked around the corner of the building to join me. Slowly he circled the little car twice.

"No bullet marks."

"I told you that I didn't hear any bullets hit."

"Doesn't that strike you as odd?"

"Odd? He missed me, that's all."

"Even the lousiest marksman should have been able to hit a target as large as a car."

"And so?"

"And so I don't think he was trying to hit you."

Bone-tired and still somewhat frightened, I felt an exasperated impulse to fly at him and start kicking his shins. Instead I asked, "Then why did he fire at me?"

"To frighten you."

"Why should he have wanted to do that?"

"As a prank, maybe. Maybe some kid thought it might be fun to give the Eastern lady a taste of the Old West."

"I don't believe any kid—"

"Why not? You're an attractive young woman. Some teenager with no hope of making an impression on you any other way might pull a stunt like that."

"Oh, knock it off, Mr. Farrel! You may be right about someone firing those shots just to frighten me. But it wasn't any prank. Whoever did it knows I'm out here. And he's afraid that I'm going to succeed. He's afraid that I'll be able to prove that your father railroaded the wrong man to prison."

I knew that wasn't quite fair, but I had been unable to resist the desire to lash out at him, in one way or another. I had expected his face to turn cold and hard. Instead, after a moment, he said quietly, "Nobody tried to railroad him. The evidence was there, and my father gathered it, that's all." He broke off and then said, "You look awful, do you know that?"

Wanting to burst into tears, I snapped, "I've got a right to look awful."

"I was going to suggest that we both drive out to that shack. But you've told me enough that I'll know where to look for bullets and shell casings and tire tracks. As for you, I think you'd better go back to the hotel."

He was right. In another moment I might find myself crumpled up at his feet.

"I hope you find something," I said sullenly, and got into the Datsun.

CHAPTER
SIXTEEN

DESPITE MY FATIGUE, I had not expected to be able to fall asleep. But within a minute or two after I removed my denim dress and lay down on my hotel room bed, I lost consciousness.

The phone's ringing brought me awake to reddish sunset light. I reached out and lifted the phone from its cradle.

Ben Farrel said, "You feeling better?"

"Yes." In fact, my nap had refreshed me considerably. "Did you find anything?"

"Some tire tracks that look recent, and one shell casing. No bullets. He must have gathered them up. How he missed the shell casing I don't know." He paused. "You could come to the office now. Or would you like to have dinner with me? We could discuss everything then.''

I found I liked the idea, which, considering how furious I had been with him only a couple of hours ago, was surprising indeed.

"Here at the hotel?"

"No, we can do better than that. There's a place about fifteen miles from here, near the interstate highway. It's quite famous for its food."

"Maybe we should make it the hotel after all. I didn't bring any clothes suitable for really fancy dining."

He laughed. "Don't worry about that. This place near the highway is good, especially if you like barbecue, but it's no Lutèce."

I wondered how he knew about the Lutèce. He went on, "That blue dress you had on today would fit right in."

So he had noticed what I wore. That too pleased me. "No, I think I know what I'll wear." The pink chemise and gray shawl I had worn to the Gainsworths should do very nicely.

"Okay. Could you be ready about seven?"

"Yes." I hesitated and then said, "Shall we go in my car?"

"Why?"

"Well, it just struck me that you might be planning to use a police car, and I'd feel rather conspicuous in that."

Again he laughed. "I'll be driving my own car if you'll settle for a beat-up Mustang. Oh, one thing more, so I can add it to my notes before I leave the office. Who can you think of who knew you were going out to that arroyo today?"

"Well, Lawrence Gainsworth knew." Briefly I told him about having dinner with the Gainsworths.

"And this afternoon before I went out to the arroyo I asked a woman in Beersheba for directions. And earlier, as I'm sure you know, I dropped by your office and asked Mrs. Canby the same thing. So I guess almost anyone could have known where I was going."

He said dryly, "How right you are."

My pulse quickened. "Then you've decided it wasn't just some teenage prankster?"

"I haven't decided anything, not yet. Well, see you at seven."

The Mustang, small, persimmon-colored, and sporty, was several years old, but not in the least beat-up. We drove past the bank, and the luncheonette, and the movie theater (Lash LaRue in *The Sagebrush Kid*), and the Jay-Bee Service Station. Out on the county road we passed the McCabe house, the scabrous patches on its green facade invisible in the darkness, and then, about ten minutes later, past the tiny house where I had spent the first three years of my life.

Ben said, "About the guy who shot at you. As I told you, I found a shell casing. Not that it helps much."

I looked at him. He had exchanged his khaki uniform for gray slacks and a gray turtleneck and a blue blazer. In the upward-striking light from the dashboard his bony face was unsmiling, even a little worried looking. Why? Had he, in spite of what he told me over the phone, decided that the shots fired at me could not have been somebody's idea of a joke? Or was he still just worried about his father?

I said, "Why doesn't the casing help?"

"Because it belonged to a twenty-two caliber bullet. Almost every male around here over the age of twelve owns a twenty-two." He paused. "As for the tracks, they don't help much either."

"Where were the tracks?"

"Running between the road and the shed

behind the lean-to. Evidently someone had driven a Jeep or pickup truck in there. Then he went into the lean-to and waited for you."

Again I thought, with a shrinking sensation in my stomach, about how near I had come to stopping my car and going into the lean-to. "Why don't the tracks help?"

"Because I could make out from the tread patterns that the tires had been Armstrong Two Tracks. Nearly everybody around here with a Jeep or pickup, or camper, and that means most of the population, uses that brand of tire.

"Of course," he went on, "if the tire prints were in clay or mud, I'd be able to take casts of them. That way I might pick up individual characteristics, such as worn spots, which could help me identify them. But that doesn't work in soil this hard and dry. The prints were so faint that I wouldn't even have noticed them if I hadn't been looking for them."

"Then you don't think there's much chance of your finding the man?"

"I'm afraid not. Not unless we get a lucky break. Of course, my deputies and I will keep asking around, trying to find someone who saw an RV turn off the

Beersheba road that day." After a moment he went on, "But at least there's one thing I'm convinced of. Whoever the man was who fired those shots, he wasn't trying to kill you."

"But how on earth can you be so—"

"If he'd wanted to kill you, he'd have followed you to the arroyo. He'd have made sure that you were dead, and then driven away. He wouldn't have shot at you while you were in a moving car, especially not with a twenty-two. It isn't very accurate at a distance of more than a hundred feet or so."

I realized he was right. How easy it would have been for someone to creep up on me as I sat there on the grass in the little canyon, daydreaming or perhaps even asleep. I said, with an inward shudder, "Then you feel sure he was just trying to frighten me, either as a joke, or because he feels threatened by my—snooping around."

After a long moment he said, "I suppose it could be connected with Joe Hartley." His tone was sober. "It doesn't seem likely, after twenty years, but it's possible."

I felt his gaze on my face. "Look, Deborah." It was the second time he'd used my first name. "Why don't you try to forget it all for just a few hours?" He switched on the car's radio. In his time-roughened but still moving baritone, Frank Sinatra announced that he intended to shake those little town blues and head for New York. "You look as if you could use a little relaxation."

After a moment he added, "I've been meaning to ask you. How are they treating you at the hotel?"

"I have the best room in the house, they tell me."

He laughed. "That must be the second floor corner room with the barbed-wire wallpaper." When I looked at him inquiringly he went on, "I made a drug bust in that room once. A couple of fellows came across the border in one of those low-flying planes and had to crash land in the desert, just before dawn. I guess because they didn't know what else to do, they hiked to Prosperity and registered at the hotel. The desk clerk called us and said two pretty disheveled-looking guys had shown up with one suitcase between them and a story about their plane running out of gas. When they learned there was no car rental place in town, they'd offered to buy the clerk's car. My father went out looking for the plane, and I came to the hotel. There were almost two pounds of pure heroin in the suitcase.''

He added, ''The Hotel Hotchkiss is pretty beat up now, but in its day, back when the mines were open and Prosperity was really prosperous, it was considered one of the finest in the West. Lily Langtry once stayed there, maybe right in your room, although it must have looked very different then— flocked wallpaper, probably, and gas lamps and maybe a four-poster with a canopy.''

''Lily Langtry? Really?''

''Yes. Prosperity had an opera house in those days, right where the movie is now. She performed there.''

''Were any of your people here then?''

''Oh, yes. My great-grandfather came out here from Virginia right after the Civil War. He was a surveyor.''

With the radio playing softly in the background, he went on talking about New Mexico in his great-grandfather's day. I knew that he sought to distract me from my anxieties, and he succeeded. I found myself enjoying his stories, and the muted music and, through the car's right-hand window, the sight of the Dog Star following the Hunter up the indigo sky.

After that quiet drive, the restaurant, even from the outside, gave an impression of liveliness and noise. The parking lot was packed. On a huge neon sign, the words "Ray's Roundup" alternated with the image of a booted and fringe-skirted cowgirl, whirling a lasso above her ten-gallon hat. When we entered we were greeted by the sound of a four-piece band—piano, drums, banjo, and guitar—playing "The Yellow Rose of Texas." I saw that Ben must have intended for us to talk, because the reserved table to which a waiter led us was on the opposite side of the room from that amplified band.

He had been right about the informality of the place. The men, almost without exception, wore cowboy boots with their jeans or chinos. If they wore ties at all, they were of the Western string variety. The women went in for "prairie" clothes—skirts and blouses and dresses of denim or flowered cotton.

When the waiter had brought our rum and sodas and then gone away, I said, "You were right about my denim dress. I feel a little out of place here in this."

He looked surprised. "You? Out of place? Why, you make everyone else look

194

out of place."

It was an awkward compliment, but I could tell he meant it.

Ben also had been right about the hearty Tex-Mex food. It was excellent—barbecued beef accompanied by some dish of mixed vegetables that tasted like ratatouille but probably was something else. With it we drank a very good California Burgundy.

About midway through the meal Ben asked, "Have you ever been to that Pakistani restaurant in Chelsea? It's on Eighteenth Street, between Seventh and Eighth Avenues, I think. Of course, maybe it isn't still there."

I said, "It's there. But how on earth did you know about it?"

"Two years ago I spent ten months in New York."

"Doing what?"

"Taking a postgraduate course at the Police Academy."

"The Police Academy!"

"Yes. Even when I was a liberal arts student at the University of New Mexico I knew what I really wanted to be was a cop. It's in the blood, I guess. I don't mean just my dad. *His* dad was a chief of police too, only in those days he was called sheriff.

Anyway, I served as my dad's deputy for a couple of years. Then I heard that the New York Police Academy was looking for college graduates from all over the country to study for advanced degrees in criminology. I applied, and they accepted me. I'd probably be a New York detective right now if my dad hadn't got sick."

"You felt you had to come home?"

"Yes. I had to hold down his job for him if I could. Maybe you don't think of small towns as having politics, but they do, and pretty nasty politics sometimes. For years the mayor has been trying to get my father out of office, but Dad kept getting reelected. When Dad had his stroke, I was sure the mayor would feel this was his chance. He could put on pressure for Dad to resign. So I came home. Dad was still in the hospital then, but be was able to swear me in as acting chief. Ever since I've been holding down his job for him."

After a moment I asked, "Did you like New York?"

"Hell, yes! Who wouldn't like a place where at three in the morning, if you've a mind to, you can draw money out of the bank, fill a prescription, buy a plane ticket to Europe, or eat a full-course restaurant meal? Oh, I got homesick for New Mexico. Twice during those ten months I splurged on a weekend trip home. But after I'd seen Dad, and filled my lungs with New Mexico air, it was good to get back to New York."

"About your father. Has he learned yet that I'm out here?"

"Yes. He mentioned it last night. I had hoped to keep it from him, but I suppose someone was bound to tell him before long."

"Then he knows—"

"The reason you came here? Yes."

"How did he take it?"

"Not the way I feared. Funny how wrong you can be about another person, even your own parent."

"But what did he say?"

"He said, 'Poor little tyke.' That sounded odd to me, of course, but when he last saw you you were three years old. Then he said, 'I never wanted to believe Joe Hartley was guilty. I had to because of the evidence, but I sure hated to see him go to prison. Maybe someone like her can get him out. If so, more power to her.' "

"What did he mean, someone like me?"

"He meant someone rich. Someone who could hire the best detectives. Someone who

197

had Washington connections maybe, and that way could put pressure on the parole board. By the way, why haven't you hired detectives and put on some pressure at the state capital and so on? Why don't you use some clout?''

''Because I don't have any. And I've got no money to speak of, either.''

He looked at me incredulously. ''But how can that be? The story in Prosperity has been that your mother married a multi-millionaire. And once a few years ago your mother was in a TV documentary the network showed out here. It was about the Hamptons, and in one shot it showed your mother and your stepfather playing tennis on their private court.''

''I know.'' I'd still been at Radcliffe when that documentary was made. ''But my stepfather's dead now. And although my mother and I didn't know it, he'd ceased to be rich quite a while before his death.

''Oh, I'm not going to have to go on relief,'' I added, ''But if I lost my job and by any chance couldn't find another one, it wouldn't be long before I became hard up indeed.''

His face had taken on an expression I found absolutely unreadable. After a moment he said, "Well, I'm sorry." Perhaps he might have said more, but the waiter came just then to take our order for dessert. After that heavy entrée, all either of us wanted was lemon sherbet and coffee. We finished dessert. Then I went to the rest room, repaired my lipstick, and came back. I had expected to find Ben with the check in front of him; instead I saw a fresh bottle of wine on the table.

He said, "After the next set a couple of ballad singers will take over from the band. They're good. I thought you might like to stay for a while and listen to them."

The singers, first a man and then a woman, were indeed good, or at least seemed so to me. Perhaps it is because of the strong Celtic strain in my own heritage—that young couple who drowned in the arroyo were both of Scottish descent—that I find Country and Western music so moving. It seems to me that the people who write these modern ballads must have some ancestral memory of Scotland: its wild moors and lonely valleys, its blood feuds, its faithless lovers, and its star-crossed ones. The only real difference is that the hero of the Country and Western ballad rides, not on a shaggy Highland pony, but on a ten-ton trailer truck, and the lover betrays his childhood sweetheart, not with a beautiful witch encountered beside a loch, but with a barmaid in a roadside tavern.

The man sang "Lonesome Roads" in a nasal and yet pleasing voice, and several songs I had never heard before, including one about a divorced father searching for his runaway son. Then a woman sat on the high barstool in the spotlight, cradling a guitar in her arms and with her dark hair falling over one shoulder. She began to sing, in a soft contralto, "Help Me Make It Through the Night."

"Take the ribbon from my hair—"

Suddenly my throat tightened. I thought beyond this moment to the long night ahead of me in that hotel room. The memories of Greg that would overwhelm me once I lay alone in the dark. Greg lying tan and muscular beside me on the beach in East Hampton. His handsome face smiling at me across a restaurant table. His arms holding me close, his breath warm in my ear.

Ben said, "What is it?"

"That song," I tried to smile, tried to make a joke of it. 'You see, I just lost my fella." But my smile broke and so did my voice.

"Excuse me," I said, getting to my feet. "I'd better go to the ladies'—"

He stood up and caught my arm. "If you're going to cry, use my shoulder. Don't go in there where I can't follow you. Go get in the car. I'll be with you as soon as I've paid the check."

Seated in the Mustang in the dark parking lot, I managed to get control of myself. Ben came out and got behind the wheel. About two miles down the road he drove into a rest stop and turned off the ignition, "All right. Tell me about it."

"There was this man. We were perfect for each other. At least he was perfect for me. We were engaged. Then I found out about my father. Until then I hadn't known. You see, my mother hadn't wanted me to— But never mind all that. Once I knew my father was in prison I had to tell Greg. He still wanted to marry me. I'm sure that even now he does. But he can't. He called me last night to tell me so."

Ben said explosively, "Why in hell can't he?"

"His family," I said in a dull voice. "His future. He has so much that would be badly affected if he married a convict's daughter.''

Ben remained silent, but I could guess what he was thinking.

''You don't understand,'' I said. ''He isn't being unfair, or snobbish, or anything like that. He didn't know about my father when he asked me to marry him. That means it would be unfair for me to try to hold onto him now. But, oh, it hurts so much. And that song, that sad, sad song—''

The tears I had thought were under control burst from me again. He gathered me close. For a while I wept wildly against his shoulder, not just for Greg but for so much else that had changed in my once pleasant life. Gradually my tears subsided. I mopped my face with the handkerchief he had taken from his pocket. He tilted my chin then and kissed me.

The touch of that warm, firm mouth was comforting. Then after a few seconds it became something more than comforting. My arms tightened around his neck. His mouth, leaving mine, touched my throat. Then abruptly he unclasped my arms from around his neck and gently put me away from him.

He said, a trifle unsteadily, ''That

doesn't mean I don't think you're attractive. You're very attractive. But you're a smashed-up lady who also has had quite a lot to drink. Call me a throwback, or a sagebrush Galahad, or just a plain sap, but in my book there are rules about how you treat a lady in your situation."

He turned the ignition key. When we'd driven half a mile or so I said, "Thank you. My life is mixed up enough right now without my taking on further complications."

"So I figured."

Again we drove in silence. Then I asked, "Have you got a girl, Ben?"

"Not a girl. I date a girl here in town, and a couple of others over in Bolton."

"Have you ever been engaged?"

"Oh, sure. I almost married my childhood sweetheart."

"What happened?"

"Well, by the time we got around to making marriage plans, we found we'd known each other so long that being together was a real drag."

Neither of us spoke for a while. Then he said, "Deborah, I want you to go home."

My tears had relieved a lot of my tension. I said, feeling a little light-headed, "Still trying to run me out of town, Chief?"

"I mean it, Deborah."

"You could use a floater. In TV shows they're always saying that someone got run out of town on a floater. Maybe if you looked around your office you could find one, whatever it is."

He said impatiently, "It's a vagrancy charge, which isn't put into effect unless the accused fails to leave town. Don't joke. I'm serious about this."

"I'm serious too, Ben. I'm not leaving. not yet. For one thing I'm going up to the prison on the regular visiting day, day after tomorrow. Anyway, if it's all right with your father for me to be here, I don't see why you—"

"Then let me put it this way. Whether or not what happened to you this afternoon was a prank, I don't want it to happen again. Next time you might get hit. For the time being it's me, not my father, who's charged with keeping order in this town, and there's nothing quite as disorderly as a young woman lying out in the desert with a few bullet holes in her."

I flinched. He said, "Sorry. But I have to make you understand what you may be risking."

"I already understand. But if I run now, I'll lose whatever chance I might have had of proving that my father doesn't belong where he is. He'll die in prison, Ben, he'll die there. I can't let that happen, not if there's any way at all of preventing it."

Several seconds passed. Then he said heavily, "All right. But will you promise me something? Don't go driving alone after dark. And don't go driving along desert side roads even in the daytime. If there is some reason you feel you have to go to that arroyo again, or even to Beersheba, let me know. I'll go with you, or send one of my deputies."

"All right. I promise." After a moment I said, "Speaking of your deputies, did either you or your deputy recognize that robber they were holding over in Bolton?"

"No. The man they'd arrested was not the same one who held up the luncheonette here in Prosperity."

We had entered the town now. As we neared the hotel he said, "My father would like to see you. Since I can't get you to leave, could you spare him a few minutes tomorrow morning?"

"Gladly." I'd wondered about the man whose evidence had put my father behind bars for life.

"I'll pick you up around ten. We can walk there. It's only a few doors off Main Street."

He stopped the Mustang at the curb and turned toward me, his face dimly visible in the light from the hotel lobby. By his expression, rueful and yet not entirely displeased, I knew he was thinking about my refusal to leave town.

"Get some sleep," he said. He accompanied me across the sidewalk and said good night at the lobby door.

CHAPTER
SEVENTEEN

THAT NIGHT WASN'T too bad. Not good, but not nearly as bad as the night before. True, I tossed and turned for a couple of hours, trying to evade thoughts of Greg. But when I finally fell asleep I did not dream of him. When I awoke around eight, I felt reasonably refreshed.

Again I breakfasted at the luncheonette. When I emerged from it, I saw Lawrence Gainsworth's sedan standing at the curb in front of the grocery next door. The young Mexican, Enrique, who'd driven me up to the Gainsworth house, was loading tall bags of groceries into the car's trunk. He smiled and said, "Good morning, Miss Channing."

I returned his greeting and then went into

the hotel and up to my room.

At ten Ben Farrel called me from the lobby. We walked along Main Street to the movie theater and then turned onto a wide street bordered by cottonwoods. The Farrel house, the fifth one from the corner, was a two-story white frame with a turret and a wraparound porch. It looked as if it might have wandered out to New Mexico from Ohio around the turn of the century. Its lawn, though, like that of other houses along the street, was not a lush Ohio green but light brown. That was because it was made of zoysia grass, Ben told me, a spreading plant that could survive in an arid climate, but did not turn green until after the soaking spring rains. Around the house's foundation, in place of low evergreens, was a border of barrel and prickly pear cactus.

On the shadowed porch Ben turned the handle of the old-fashioned bell. "Mrs. Galstrup wants everyone to ring, including me, even though the door's always unlocked."

"Mrs. Galstrup?"

"She's the nurse-housekeeper. She took care of my mother eight years ago during her last illness, so when Dad had his stroke

I rehired her.''

She opened the door, a middle-aged woman with a pleasant smile but an authoritative glint in her eye. When Ben had made the introductions she said, "Please don't keep him talking long."

She ushered us onto a big screened porch. Ben's father, a man of sixty or a little less, sat in a white wicker armchair, a brown blanket over his knees. Despite the slight droop at the right side of his mouth, he was a good-looking man, with bright blue eyes set in a face that, not too many years ago, probably had been more conventionally handsome than his son's.

He said, smiling at me, "Three years old, and holding a teddy bear with a missing ear. Even then I could tell you were going to favor your mother. But there's the look of your father, too, around your eyes and mouth. Have a seat, and forgive me for not getting up. My right leg's still gimpy."

Ben and I sat down in wicker chairs facing him. He said, "I hear you've been to see your father."

I nodded.

"How is he?"

"He says he's fine." My throat tightened. "But he looks sort of—bleached out."

"I know what you mean. It's a look some men get after they've been in prison a number of years. I suppose you're going to see him again."

"Yes, tomorrow."

"Will you tell him something for me? Tell him all the time it was happening back there twenty years ago, I kept praying that something would turn up to demolish the evidence against him. Tell him I still hope that."

"I will."

"Since you've been out here, has anything happened? Anything that might be evidence in Joe's favor, I mean?"

On the brief walk over from the hotel, Ben had told me he did not want his father to know about those rifle shots. I said, "Well, I visited Loretta McCabe. Her mother sneaked out to my car afterwards and said she was sure it was Ed Smith who'd killed her granddaughter. Ed Smith is Loretta's—"

"I know who he is. I should. I've had to pick him up off the sidewalk and drive him home often enough. What reason did Mrs. Carruthers give you for suspecting Ed?"

"No real reason. She'd taken his army discharge out of his bureau drawer to show me that his middle name was Joseph. And she says that he hated Daisy, and my father, too. Something about a row over a stolen tire.''

''I wonder when she dreamed up this theory. Certainly she didn't say anything about it at the time of the trial.'' He paused. ''The old lady's balmy, you know.''

''Yes, I guessed that.''

''Living with Loretta and Ed,'' Ben said, ''who wouldn't turn balmy?''

Mrs. Galstrup came out onto the porch and said, with a meaningful look at Ben and me, ''Medicine time!''

Ben and I stood up. I said, ''I hope you're entirely well soon.''

''Oh, I will be! I'm feeling stronger every day. And with Ben here to act as my deputy, I'll be able to hold down my job as well as I ever did.''

Well, what had I expected? If Ben cared enough for his father to leave the New York Police Academy, it wasn't surprising that he would plan to stay here and help his father hold down his job when he went back to work. Anyway, what concern was it of mine if Ben chose to spend the rest of his life in this hamlet?

Out on the sidewalk I said, "I like your father very much."

"Yes, he's quite a guy." He paused and then asked, "What are you going to do this afternoon? Not wander around, I hope."

"I'm going to stay in my room and wash my hair and read *Gone With the Wind.*"

Before my plane left New York I'd seen a paperback edition of the novel on sale at the airport bookshop. Despite its considerable heft, I had bought it and placed it in my carry-on tote bag.

"Good," Ben said, and then added, "I'm going to be pretty busy today, and this evening I'd better do paper work. Damned State Attorney General's office keeps sending questionnaires to be filled out. But I could spare an hour or two for dinner at the hotel. How about it?"

Why not? True, I knew now that he would offer no enduring refuge for—to use his phrase—a smashed-up lady. Once I left this little town it was highly improbable that I would ever see him again. But in the meantime—well, why deprive myself of having dinner with an attractive man?

I said, "I'd like that."

"We'll have pot roast. That's always safe."

Wondering at Southwesterners' insatiable appetite for beef, I said good-bye to him outside Town Hall and then walked to the hotel. I spent the rest of the afternoon in my room with my hair dryer and Scarlett and Rhett.

From six-thirty to eight Ben and I sat in the hotel dining room, eating good pot roast and practically tasteless vegetables, and speculating about what the dining room had looked like when Lily Langtry stayed at this hotel. In those days had the same animal heads—deer and desert fox and snarling wildcat—stared down with glass eyes from the walls? And what about the help? We decided that in those days, instead of one bunion-afflicted waitress who shuffled back and forth between the few occupied tables and the kitchen, there must have been hordes of mustached waiters in white shirtfronts and tailcoats.

He went back to his office, and I went up to my room and the Battle of Atlanta. I read until the print blurred before my eyes. When I went to sleep I again, mercifully, did not dream of Greg, but of grubbing alongside Scarlett and her sisters for roots in a deserted field. It had a windbreak of junipers, just like the fields at Beersheba.

I came downstairs the next morning feeling calmer than I had for quite a while. Perhaps that was why I found the letter the day clerk handed to me especially shocking.

He said, with his slight stammer, "Post office sent it over about ten minutes ago." His eyes held curiosity, which wasn't surprising, because the blue envelope looked odd indeed. Its address—Deborah Channing, Hotchkiss Hotel, Prosperity, New Mexico—had been printed in red pencil. Its strokes were thick and oily-looking, almost like that of a crayon. I turned the envelope over. No return address. Aware of the clerk's gaze following me, I walked about twenty feet away from the desk. Back turned to him, I opened the envelope. The brief message inside was not printed. Instead the sender had scissored out words from newspapers or magazines—from both, to judge by the varying texture of the paper on which they had been printed—and placed them on blue notepaper.

The message read:

Hello there, Jailbird's daughter. I wish you lots of luck.

Joe.

With a sense of unreality, I stared down at it. I had read newspaper accounts of anonymous letter writers—senders of ransom notes, for instance—who had used this device to try to make sure their communications could not be traced, but I had never expected to hold such a missive in my hand.

Then the full impact of it hit me. He was still out there someplace. Joe, the man for whose hideous crime my father had spent twenty years shut up in that gray place.

I kept looking at the page. He had made the punctuation marks—the comma after "there" and the periods after "daughter" and "luck"—with that same thick red pencil. Irrelevantly, I wondered how many books or magazines or newspapers he had mutilated to compose that brief, mocking message. Quite a few, undoubtedly. Almost every word was in a different typeface. And one word, "Jailbird's," was in two typefaces, the first syllable looking as if it came from a newspaper subhead, the last syllable much smaller and printed on the slick paper many magazines use.

I again looked at the envelope and saw for the first time that its postmark was

"Prosperity, N.M." So it had been mailed right here in town. I placed the message back in the envelope, feeling frightened and a little sick, because he surely was crazy, this Joe, not only to have done what he did twenty years ago, but to compose and send the message I held in my hand. At the same time, I felt exultant. Here was proof that when little Daisy prattled about Joe she spoke of a real human being, not of an imaginary person or even animal, as Loretta McCabe had suggested.

I hurried out into the sunlight and down the street to Town Hall. I found Ben unlocking the door of police headquarters. He took one look at me and said, "What is it?" Then, as I started to answer: "No, tell me inside."

We walked through the deserted outer office and into the private one. I handed him the envelope. "The clerk said it was delivered about ten minutes ago."

Ben shot me a quizzical look and then opened the blue envelope and took out the message. After a moment he restored the page to the envelope and laid it on his desk.

"I'm sorry to disappoint you, but this time it *really* looks like kid stuff."

"Kid stuff!" Instantly I knew it did look

like that, but nevertheless I protested, "How would a kid, even one in his late teens, know about Joe? I mean, how would he know that Loretta McCabe testified that Daisy kept talking about someone named Joe?"

"He couldn't remember the trial, of course. But people have talked about the case down through the years. Nothing like Daisy McCabe's death had ever happened in this town before. Besides—"

He broke off, and then asked, "How many people have you talked with about that aspect of the case? I mean, about Loretta McCabe's testimony that her little girl talked of someone named Joe?"

"Loretta herself, of course. And her mother."

"No one else? Did you mention it to anyone during your two visits to the colony at Beersheba?"

"Perhaps. Yes, I think I did, although I'm not sure whether it was to Mr. or Mrs. Jenkins or Nathaniel Crisp."

"Did you talk about it to the Gainsworths when you had dinner up there?"

"No, I'm positive I didn't."

"Well, I've got a strong hunch who

pulled this little stunt. Loretta McCabe is pretty chummy with another divorcee. Trudie Clayton, who lives a few doors from her. Trudie has a seventeen-year-old son. Malcolm Clayton is the worst kid in town. Shoplifting, drunk driving, killing songbirds with an air rifle, you name it. He did a year at a state school for boys, but it didn't seem to change him any.''

I thought of the boy sauntering up the walk to that tan stucco house with an air rifle under his arm. ''Does he have one of those Red Indian haircuts?''

''That's our Malcolm. Where did you see him?''

I told him. ''And you believe he sent this?''

''I'd almost bet on it. He could very well have overheard Loretta McCabe telling his mother about your visit. He could have gotten the idea of pasting printed words on a page from something he saw on TV. He spends at least twice as much time sitting in front of the TV set as he does in his high school classes.

''And here's another thing. The quality of the letter paper. It's pretty good, the best you can buy here at the Prosperity Drug Store, anyway. I know, because I once bought a box of this kind of paper to give to a girl.'' Fleetingly I wondered who the girl was. ''Malcolm's mother wouldn't be apt to buy that grade of paper, but Malcolm might very well have stolen it.'' He added dryly, ''He's a very discriminating thief. Always takes the best brand of sardines off the grocery shelf and the most expensive bicycle out of the rack.''

I said, unwilling to be convinced, ''But you haven't proved anything!''

''No.''

''And even though this does seem like something a juvenile delinquent would do— Well, some people remain juvenile all their lives.''

''I know. My theory about Malcolm Clayton may be all wrong, I just gave you my first reaction. Now wait here. I'm going to the post office and see if they have any idea just when this was mailed.''

When he had gone I sank into a straight chair and stared at a photograph of Monument Valley on a calendar on the wall. I had to agree, however reluctantly, that the message I'd received seemed like the product of a juvenile personality. On the other hand, couldn't it have been some

219

mature person imitating the act of a teenager?

Suddenly I thought of John Whitecloud's middle-aged face peering through the window of that deserted little house. But no. Probably he couldn't even read. Certainly it was hard to imagine him scissoring out bits of newsprint and pasting them onto a piece of letter paper.

Ben came back and closed the office door behind him. "It was mailed sometime between seven-thirty yesterday morning and seven-thirty this morning. You see, it was deposited in that mailbox outside the post office. That box is opened once a day at seven-thirty A.M."

"Then people at the post office remember that particular envelope?"

"Oh, yes. As you can imagine, the volume of mail here in Prosperity isn't very heavy. Besides, the envelope was addressed to you, the stranger in town, and the writer had used red pencil to print your name. So of course they remembered that the envelope was among the mail taken from the outside box, not from the letter drop inside the post office."

"But they have no idea who—"

"No. And no idea when it was mailed,

except that it had to be sometime during the night.''

''Is there a chance of finding finger-prints?''

''Not much. The envelope has been handled by a number of people besides the one who sent it—you, me, the hotel clerk, the post-office people. As for the message inside, I've got a hunch that anyone who went to the trouble of hiding his identity with bits of newsprint would also take the trouble to avoid leaving fingerprints on the page. Besides all that, paper doesn't take fingerprints very well.

''But I'll do my best,'' he went on. ''I'll take it over to Bolton today. They've got a pretty good lab there. They ought to be able not just to pick up any fingerprints, but to tell me whether or not I'm right about the brand of letter paper that was used. And later today or perhaps tomorrow I'll make a call on Malcolm's mother and see if there's paper of that sort on the premises.''

''But will she let you—''

''Probably. I doubt that I'll even have to prepare a search warrant. The poor woman's used to cops showing up to ask questions about Malcolm. Now what about you? Had breakfast yet?''

I shook my head. "I'll stop someplace on the way. I want to get started to the prison."

"Just be sure you do stop. Are you going to tell your father about this message?"

"Of course not, nor about those rifle shots either. I don't want him to be worried about me any more than he is already."

Ben nodded. "Keep your mind on your driving, Deborah. And just—watch out for yourself."

Perhaps he did feel that most likely I was the target only of some comparatively harmless juvenile. But it seemed to me that there was genuine worry in his face.

"I'll watch out." I went through the outer office, where Dot Canby was now typing and Deputy Hal Newby stood looking through a filing cabinet. Out on the sidewalk, I turned toward the hotel and my rented Datsun.

CHAPTER
EIGHTEEN

TODAY THAT LONG room with the plate-glass partition seemed filled to capacity. Except for one elderly man, the visitors were all women—black women, white women, Indian women, some young, some old, some middle-aged.

The prisoners on the opposite side of the barrier showed the same racial and age range. Several were about my father's age or older. The one seated opposite the lone male visitor—the old man's grandson?—looked to be no more than twenty.

My father said, "I hoped you'd have gone back to New York by now." But his expression was saying something quite different.

"Papa, I told you I'd be here the next

visiting day."

"Well, I've got to admit that I've been looking forward to it, even though I was hoping, in another way, that you'd have left." He paused, "What've you been doing, a big-city girl like you, in that pokey little town?"

"Seeing people. People who sent you messages."

"What people?"

The eagerness in his eyes made my heart twist. How hungry he must be for any sort of contact with those who once had been his neighbors and friends. "Jay Barnwell, the gas station owner, sent you his regards."

"Good old Jay. We used to go hunting together. How did he seem?"

"Fine." I hesitated and then went on, "He said that it wasn't for lack of wanting to that he's never come to see you."

"I know. It's been his wife, Bee. All the women were up in arms about the case, especially the mothers. Nobody could blame them for that."

I wondered, feeling sick, if some of them had gathered outside during the trial to yell and shake their fists at him as he was brought to and from the courtroom.

I said hurriedly, "And of course

Lawrence Gainsworth sent you his regards. He's also mailing you some more books."

He said, sounding pleased, "So you got together with Lawrence."

"Yes, and I liked him a lot." I told him about my pleasant evening at that big house in the hills. "I liked his daughter, too, even though she's a bit odd. She flared up at her father all of a sudden over a painting of hers. He'd liked it, but after she finished it she disliked it so much she destroyed it."

He said, "Rachel always was a bit strange. I suppose it's artistic temperament. But anyway, speaking of Lawrence, I've got something I'd like you to take to him. Or rather, the trusty in the warden's outer office has it.

"You see, I'm allowed to send out only two pieces of mail a month. And so I figured that if you *did* show up here today, I'd ask you to get it to Lawrence, one way or another. The warden's a good guy. He'll bend the rules a little sometimes. Of course, he'll have censored it. Anything that goes out of here is censored."

"But what *is* it?"

"It's a photostatic copy of two chapters of a book by William Cobbett. Ever hear of him?"

"Never."

He said, gently teasing, "And you a Radcliffe graduate! Cobbett was a nineteenth-century English journalist who wrote something called *Rural Rides,* all about farming and farm workers in his day. He was a funny old bird with lots of crank notions, but he did have some amazingly modern ideas about crop rotation and so on.

"Anyway, Lawrence mentioned in one of his letters that he wanted to quote to me from Cobbett, who's been long out of print, of course, but found his copy of *Rural Rides* was no longer readable. He'd left it out on the terrace, and a rainstorm had come up. Anyway, a copy has turned up in a box of books donated to the prison library. I can't send him the book, of course. But he'd said he was sure that the quote he'd wanted to send was somewhere in the first two chapters, so I photostated them."

"I'll be glad to take them. As it happens, Rachel is going to phone me tomorrow about our having lunch together."

"Maybe you'd like to read Cobbett before you hand him over to Lawrence." He smiled. "That way I could feel that I've contributed to my daughter's education."

"Oh, Papa! If it weren't for you I wouldn't be on this earth to get an education."

"Well, I can't dispute that. Now who else sent messages?"

I said, after a moment's hesitation, "Mr. Farrel. Ben Farrel, Senior, I mean. He said that before the trial and all through it, and afterward, he kept hoping something would turn up to wipe out all his evidence against you."

My father said softly, "I always had a lot of respect for Ben Farrel." Then: "Any more messages?"

"No. But I did go to see Loretta McCabe. She wasn't—any help. But her mother followed me out to my car and said she thought Ed Smith was the—the one who killed Daisy. Maybe you remember Ed Smith. He's—"

"I remember. But I'm surprised he and Loretta are still together."

"Mrs. Carruthers had sneaked his army discharge out of the house to prove to me his middle name was Joseph. She also said that he'd hated Daisy, and hated you, too, because of a fight over a tire Ed had stolen."

My father shook his head. "Honey, as the English say, that horse won't run. My fight with Ed was a year before Daisy was killed. And you can say one thing for alcoholics. They seldom carry grudges. It's hard for them to keep on feeling anything, including rage, from one day to the next."

I didn't answer that. He said, "What else have you been up to?"

I thought rapidly. I didn't want to tell him about Beersheba and my encounter with those unforgiving colonists, Samuel Jenkins and Nathaniel Crisp. But surely it would be all right to tell him about my trip to the little canyon where my grandparents' camper had stood.

"I drove out to see the arroyo where Mother's parents drowned. In spite of what happened there, it's a lovely spot."

He nodded. "You were there once before. When you were about fourteen months old your mother and you and I drove out there one Sunday." He added, "I'm afraid we haven't much more time, so tell me right now. When are you going back to New York?"

I didn't answer. He said gently, "Don't you see by now, honey, that you can't get me out of here? So go on back. It'a not a

228

good idea to stay away from your young man for too long."

Sooner or later I would have to tell him. "I may go back at the end of next week. But if so, it will be because I don't want to lose my job. I've already lost—I mean, Greg phoned me, and he and I decided things just wouldn't work out for us."

After a moment he said quietly, "Oh, God, I was afraid that would happen."

"Papa, don't look like that. It's not the end of the world."

He gave me a forced-looking smile. "Of course it isn't. And if the man's damn fool enough to let anything stand between him and you— Well, there are better fish in the sea than ever came out of it."

"I know," I said, although I was sure that almost any woman would say that a better fish than Gregory Vanlieden would have to be a very spectacular fish indeed.

A bell clattered, sounding like a fire alarm. "Is that—"

He nodded.

"I'll keep in touch, Papa. I'll write you right away. They don't put any limit on the letters you can receive, do they?"

He shook his head.

Behind me a guard said, "Time's up, miss."

"And if I do go back to New York next week, I'll keep writing. And I'll come out to see you every chance I get."

"Time's *up, miss."

I put my hand up against the glass and he put his hand on the other side.

"I love you, Papa."

Still he didn't speak. I knew it was because he couldn't. I got up and hurried from the room.

CHAPTER
NINETEEN

I LEFT THE prison shortly after two-thirty. Because yellow-helmeted work crews were tearing up long stretches of road, it was almost five by the time I reached Prosperity. Eager to know if Ben had learned anything about that strange letter, I phoned the police station as soon as I reached my hotel room. Dot Canby answered.

"This is Deborah Channing. Is Mr. Farrel back from Bolton yet?"

"He didn't go. Early this afternoon he was just about to leave for there, but then he got this emergency call from Chili Pepper."

"From *what?*"

"It's not a what, it's a where. A town about twenty miles south of here." She sounded a bit stiff, as if she'd heard too many Easterners make jokes about the names of New Mexican communities. "I guess you haven't heard, but a twister touched down there. No deaths reported yet, according to the radio, but half the town's gone. The mayor then asked other towns to send police and any other help they could, such as food and cots and so on."

Driving back from the prison, I'd had the radio on, and had been vaguely aware of an announcement that tornados had touched down several places near the Mexican border. But with personal problems absorbing my thoughts, I'd paid little attention to the news bulletin.

"Well, it's good there are no deaths."

"You want to leave a message for Ben?"

"Just tell him I called."

"I'll leave a note on his desk, but no telling when he'll get it. He may not be back until all hours."

I thanked her and hung up.

Until six o'clock I read the photostated copy of the first two chapters of *Rural Rides,* which had been handed to me in the warden's outer office by a stooped, gray-haired man with nicotine-stained fingers.

My father was right about William Cobbett. He had been a crotchety, cantankerous man who heaped scurrilous and often very funny abuse on his ever-widening circle of enemies. But he'd had a genuine sympathy for England's shamefully exploited farm laborers, and a genuine concern for wise use of the land, both in England and in the United States, which he visited during the first decade of the nineteenth century.

All the time I read I kept listening for the phone, but neither Ben nor anyone else called. At seven I went down to the hotel dining room. Unable to face pot roast again, I ordered breaded veal cutlets, a choice I soon regretted. The breading was grease-soaked, and the veal had the consistency and flavor of wet cardboard.

I went back to my room. I finished all the photostated pages I'd brought with me from the prison, and then turned from the turnip fields of Surrey to the forsaken cotton fields of Civil War Georgia. I went on reading Margaret Mitchell until ten-thirty. Then, sure that Ben would not call that late, I went to bed.

But not to sleep. I had no sooner turned out the light than the group of poker players of several nights before—at least I assumed it was the same ones—began to assemble in the room across the hall. Again there was loud laughter and cries of, "Which of you clowns dealt this mess?" Again someone, perhaps the desk clerk, carried trays of rattling glasses down the hall and was received with shouts of joy. Again—and this was the most infuriating of all—the noise would dwindle away to just one voice, reciting in low tones what was almost certainly a long and involved dirty story. Lulled by the near silence, I would start to drift off to sleep, only to be jerked wide-awake by brays of laughter.

At midnight I phoned the desk. No answer. I could guess why. The clerk would have known who was calling, and could be certain of the nature of my complaint, one he had no intention of acting upon. I was a stranger who probably would depart before long. The poker players were local men, regular patrons of the hotel, and perhaps generous tippers of whoever brought those trays down the hall. I began to entertain a fantasy in which I burst open the door of that room across the hall with an empty wastebasket in my hand. While the players, stunned with surprise, sat motionless, I would sweep into the basket cards, poker chips, beer cans, half-eaten sandwiches, and any money that might be lying about. Then I would cross the room and empty the basket out the window.

Around two, I felt I was on the verge of actually enacting that wastebasket fantasy. Fortunately, they all trooped noisily out of their room and headed for the elevator or perhaps the stairs. Still boiling, I did not get to sleep for at least another half hour.

The result was that I didn't wake up until after ten. I immediately called the police station.

"You've missed him again," Dot Canby said. "He's already left for Bolton."

Well, at least he was on his way to finding out what he could about that letter.

She said, "He told me to tell you that he got back from Chili Pepper so late that he was afraid he'd wake you if he called."

"Is the situation under control?"

"In Chili Pepper? Yes, but a lot of people will be sleeping on cots in the school gymnasium for a while."

"Well, please ask Mr. Farrel to phone me when he gets back from Bolton."

I had my belated breakfast at the luncheonette and then returned to the hotel. No, the day clerk told me, I'd had no calls. That was odd, I thought, as I climbed the stairs. Surely Rachel Gainsworth had said she would call me Thursday morning.

Around eleven-twenty I decided to call her. After all I had an excuse, those photostated chapters of *Rural Rides*. A woman with a Mexican accent, undoubtedly the one named Consuelo, answered the phone. Apparently, like many partially deaf people, she could hear quite well over the phone. I gave her my name, and she told me that "Miss Rachel" was in her studio.

When Rachel came on the line her voice was brisk and friendly. "Deborah! I was just about to call you." Then she must have looked at her watch, because she said, "Good Lord! Is that the right time? I'm terribly sorry. When I'm working I just lose all track of time."

"There's nothing to be sorry for. I called you because I went to the prison yesterday, and my father gave me something for Mr. Gainsworth, a photostated copy of part of a book by William Cobbett. If you like, I could just drop it in the mail."

"Certainly not! Bring it with you. We're having a picnic lunch, remember, although I'm afraid it's going to be a belated one."

"That's all right. I had a belated

breakfast. I didn't get to sleep until all hours."

I told her about the poker players. She laughed and said, "Well, you'll find it quiet enough up here. No one here but me and Consuelo and Johnny Whitecloud. Enrique has driven my father up to Gallup. As I told you, he goes there on business once a week.

"Maybe after lunch you can take a snooze under a pine tree," she went on, "Could you get here about one? I'll show you the painting I'm working on, and then we can go up to that spot I told you about, and have our lunch around two."

I felt warmed by her genuine friendliness. Once Rachel got to know a person, she wasn't shy at all. "Fine. I'll be there."

It wasn't until after I had hung up that I remembered my promise to Ben Farrel about not driving on side roads. But only the last few minutes of my journey to the Gainsworth house would be on a side road. Besides, the day I was shot at, literally scores of people—in town, and in the colony at Beersheba—could have known I would be out there in the desert. Today no one but Rachel and the Gainsworth servants would know that I would be up there in the hills—unless, of course, the desk clerk had listened in. I doubted that he had. He might listen in if I were talking to Ben Farrel or some other man. But he impressed me as the sort who would regard "women's gab" as of little interest. Feeling pleased at the thought of being once again in that spacious and lovely house, I changed from my denim dress to jeans and a sweater. I phoned Dot Canby again to ask her to tell Ben that I would be spending the afternoon with Rachel Gainsworth. "But I'd rather you didn't tell that to anyone besides Mr. Farrel."

"I won't." Her voice was rather stiff. "I keep things to myself if I'm told they're confidential."

"I'm sure you do. And thank you very much."

After I hung up I read Margaret Mitchell for a while longer, and then went down to the hotel parking lot.

CHAPTER
TWENTY

UNTIL I EMERGED from the long private road onto the edge of the large clearing around the Gainsworth house, I hadn't realized how tense I had been during the last part of my journey up here. But now, feeling my nerves relax, I knew I really had been anxious during those minutes along the narrow road, with the pine branches melting overhead to form a tunnel's roof, and with at least the possibility that someone lurked behind every tree trunk.

By contrast, the Gainsworth house and its surroundings looked welcoming indeed. Evidently at this altitude, with its heavier rainfall, a lawn of ordinary grass was feasible, at least for a millionaire. Broken only by a graveled drive, it stretched green and lush from forest wall to forest wall.

I piloted the Datsun up the driveway and stopped under the portico. It was not until I had walked to the semi-circular porch that I saw a man in jeans and a blue work shirt clipping back an ilex bush at the corner of the house. He was Johnny Whitecloud. His gaze was fixed on the clippers he wielded. Whether or not he had watched me walking to the porch I couldn't tell.

Consuelo answered the doorbell. Miss Rachel, she told me, was on the south terrace. "You want me to show you, mees?"

"No, thank you. I know where that is."

I walked down the hall and entered the dining room, with its sterling candelabra gleaming on the bare mahogany table. Through the opened French doors I could see Rachel sitting with her gaze lowered to her hands, loosely clasped in her lap. In contrast to her animated voice over the phone, her attitude now seemed strangely withdrawn and listless. I stepped out onto the terrace. "Hello, Rachel."

She turned her head, gave me a startled look, and got to her feet. She said, "Why—why, hello, Deborah."

Have you ever, while descending familiar

stairs, miscalculated the number of steps? Your foot, reaching downward for that last step, the one that isn't there, strikes jarringly against the floor. I had that same disoriented feeling as I stood there with Rachel.

I said, "Did I misunderstand? Were you inviting me for tomorrow?"

She remained silent, still looking at me with that startled expression. It occurred to me that perhaps her emotional state was even worse than her father had implied. Lord knows, I reflected, thinking of the terrified child standing on the sewing machine with a noose around her neck, there was every reason why she should have grown up into a highly disturbed woman.

I floundered on, "I would have waited for you to call *me,* except I wanted you to know I had these book chapters for your father."

Her gaze dropped to the big manila envelope I carried. "Of course. Some writer named William Cobbett, didn't you say? Deborah, you must forgive me. When you came out here onto the terrace I'd been thinking of what I'm going to do next to my painting. I call it painting in my head. And when I'm doing that I'm lost to all the world."

Her smile, like her words, was both friendly and apologetic. I relaxed. What had struck me as withdrawn, even unwelcoming, behavior had been merely artistic woolgathering.

She said, "Let's just leave that envelope on the dining room sideboard and go up to the studio. I'm dying to show you the one I'm working on now. Then I'll come back down and tell Consuelo to fix us a picnic lunch."

We went down the hall and climbed the stairs to her studio. As we entered I saw something I had not noticed the first time I was here, a door set in the far wall. By daylight the colors of the paintings lining the room seemed even more vibrant.

She flipped back the cloth covering the canvas on her easel and said, "Here's the latest. While you're looking at it, I'll go down and talk to Consuelo about lunch."

She left me. I looked admiringly at the unfinished canvas. It was another painting of the mesas, this time a deep, cool blue against a faintly flushed dawn sky.

Rachel was gone for some time. When she returned I was studying that painting of of a prickly pear cactus.

"Are we going to have a picnic!" she said. "Cucumber sandwiches and a cold lobster salad and Chablis. And Port Salut and grapes for dessert."

"Lovely!"

"How do you like my new painting?"

"Very much. As I told you the other night, I like nearly every painting here."

"Well, take your time looking. Our lunch won't be ready for a little while. Besides, I wouldn't want to hurry anyone who's looking at my pictures."

For several minutes there was silence. Arms crossed, Rachel leaned against a heavy old table that held brushes in glass jars and paint-stained rags. I moved slowly along the rows of pictures. Suddenly she said, "You want to see some really good stuff?" Her voice had taken on an odd hoarseness. "Not just paintings, but sculpture, too?"

I turned around. Her face wore a strange little smile. I said, feeling chilled but not knowing why, "What do you mean?"

"Why tell you when I can show you? Come on."

I followed her to the door set in the far side of the room. She reached up to the lintel and brought down a skeleton key. She winked at me. "I keep it locked just to remind the old man not to come in here. The last time he did, about six years ago, I raised holy hell."

I thought dazedly: "old man"? Was she talking about her father?

She unlocked the door, swung it back. I stepped past her into the room. It was another studio, smaller than the first one, but with a good north light. On the wall facing me was a grotesque Indian mask and a pair of stone-bladed tomahawks, their wooden handles crossed. A few feet away from me on a pedestal stood the bronze head of a man.

My gaze kept moving around the room. Along one wall paintings stood on the floor, their blank sides showing. In the middle of the room there was another battered table strewn with brushes in jars and paint-soaked rags. A battered old wardrobe occupied one corner. One of its doors, gaping open, revealed a green smock hanging from a hook and a pair of paint-splattered moccasins on the floor.

Evidently she was waiting for me to say something. I asked, "Did you make the mask?"

"No, that's Apache. So are the tomahawks. I've always been crazy about Indian stuff. What do you think of the bronze head?''

I looked at it more carefully and saw, with a sense of shock, that it was meant to be Lawrence Gainsworth. But she had done something to that handsome, gentle face. Somehow she had made it both weak and evil, the eyes narrowed slightly, the mouth lifted at one corner in just the suggestion of a sneer.

"It's very good," I said. Probably it was, as a work of art, but I didn't want to look at it. I asked hurriedly, "What are the paintings? Mostly landscapes?"

Instead of answering, she turned a tall canvas around to face me. It was a brutally realistic painting of a breech-clouted Indian brave, twisted features painted red and blue, tomahawk raised as he hurtled from a low mound straight down at the viewer. I knew it was only paint and canvas, but it frightened me.

"It's—it's powerful." I raised my gaze to her face. "I'm surprised to learn that you're so interested in Indian themes. One would never guess it from the other paintings."

She turned the canvas of the brave with upraised tomahawk so that it faced the wall. "What paintings?"

I said, after a dumbfounded moment, "Why, the ones in your main studio."

"You mean the girls' pictures. Hell, you call those daubs *paintings?*"

Although I already had a sickening premonition of the answer to my question, I asked, "What girls?"

"The *girls*. Oh, one of them isn't too bad a painter. Althea, the chatty one, who asked you to lunch. But Dorothy—she does mainly still lifes—she's no good. As for that poor slob Rachel, she doesn't even try very often, and when she does she turns your stomach. Cutesy-poo fawns beside forest pools, for God's sake!"

I stood motionless. I'd heard of people like this, of course. Inherently fragile individuals so abused in early childhood that they had, quite literally, shattered into personality fragments, like a walnut flying apart under a hammer's blow. But I had never expected to know such a person.

She said, "How about this one, a self-portrait? I did it—oh, several years ago."

She turned another painting around. It was indeed a self-portrait, painted from the waist up. Rachel's face looked back at me from the canvas, appearing not only somewhat younger but more masculine, the jawline heavier, the gaze bolder. She had worn a red sweater for her self-portrait and a matching knitted cap, which hid her dark hair.

I knew I should make some excuse and then get out of that house as fast as I could. Get out and drive away. Yes, even though she was only a little taller than I was, and twenty years or more older.

But there were things I desperately needed to find out, and might never find out unless I summoned up enough courage to stand my ground. And so I said, "You sent me a letter, didn't you?"

She threw me a sidewise glance. "Pretty cute, huh? I had Enrique mail it to you."

I recalled seeing the Gainsworth chauffeur in front of the grocery store, loading tall bags of food into a car's trunk. He must have mailed that grotesque missive during that trip to town.

"I wanted you to know I was still around," she said, "but I didn't want you to be able to blow the whistle on me. I mean, I don't want to find myself back in the sanitarium. The girls didn't mind so much, but I hated it. So I did the paste-up job."

That paste-up of words scissored from newspaper and magazine print, including the word Joe.

Joe, standing not four feet away from me now.

"Let me show you something that really ought to interest you." Again that wink. "The old man managed to destroy the finished portrait, but he didn't know I'd made a charcoal sketch of it before I started working on it in oil."

She stepped inside the tall wardrobe, reached up. I heard a tearing sound and knew she must be peeling some sort of gummed tape from the wardrobe ceiling. She walked back to me, uncoiling a paper cylinder, about a foot long, from which strips of transparent tape dangled. She unrolled the sketch and held it up for my inspection.

It was another self-portrait. This time the face was that of a woman in her mid-twenties. She had sketched herself wearing a sleeveless dress, but she had given her features that same subtly masculine cast. Around her neck, suspended on what looked like a leather thong, was an irregularly shaped object about the size of a large marble. Highlights suggested bits of some glinting substance imbedded in darker matter.

I knew beyond doubt that it was my father's nugget of iron pyrite, that "pocket piece" that had been found in a dead child's clenched fist.

I said, "How—how did you—"

She rolled the sketch and dropped it on the cluttered table. "You want to know about the nugget, don't you? Joe Hartley dropped it up here one day and I found it. He'd come here to fix the roof on the stables. We kept a couple of horses back then. I liked the nugget, so I painted myself wearing it. After I finished the portrait I just left the nugget lying on the table here. Then one day that damn kid tried to steal it."

I managed to say, "Daisy?"

"Yeah. She'd hitch rides with tourists passing through these hills—usually she'd tell them she had a grandmother living up here—and then walk from the highway to this house. My old man and the others would send her home. In fact, he drove her home to her mother several times. But any time she showed up while I was here and the old man was off someplace—well, I didn't mind her hanging around in here while I

249

painted. She liked to talk about Indians, too. And she always recognized me. She always knew I was Joe and not one of the girls.''

That young child, accepting with a child's matter-of-factness the idea that the Rachel who painted in this room was really a man named Joe, a friendly man who liked to talk about Indians. Or, more probably, she thought of Joe as a young boy only a few years older than herself.

I forced myself to speak. ''How did you know that the—the others didn't like Daisy?''

''Because I know everything about them! I'm the only one who knows what all the others do and think. Dorothy and Althea know about each other and about Rachel but not about me. And Rachel doesn't know about anyone but herself.'' She laughed. ''The poor slob thinks she has memory lapses!''

Frightened but fascinated, wanting to turn and run but knowing that I must not, not until I had learned what I needed to know, I said, ''So Daisy tried to steal that nugget—''

''Yes. She grabbed it and ran into the big studio. And when I chased after her and tried to get it back, she started kicking my legs. So I strangled her.''

My stomach seemed to turn over.

I could go now. I could drive down to Prosperity and tell Ben, and soon my father would be free. But first I had to think of some way of getting out of here without letting her suspect what I intended to do.

"I'd have gotten my nugget back," Rachel was saying, "if the old man hadn't come in just then. Sure, it was only a few days after he broke his arm and his collarbone, but he knocked me away from her with his good hand and then, while I was still groggy, he dragged me into this little studio and locked the door on me.

"Lord knows where my nugget is now," she added sulkily. "The cops have got it locked up someplace, I suppose."

I stretched my lips into a smile. "I suppose. Well, I'm afraid I'll have to leave now."

Her eyes narrowed. "You're going to rat on me, aren't you? You're going to have me locked up in that sanitarium."

"No, no!" Still smiling, I backed toward the doorway into the main studio. "It's just that I remembered that I should be back at the hotel. Someone's going to call me from

New York, and it's important. Well, good-bye, Rachel."

She snapped, "Don't call me that!"

"I'm sorry. Good-bye."

I turned and started toward the door that led to the hall. I heard her following footsteps.

Don't run, I warned myself. That would make her sure of her suspicions. She would pursue me. And if the front door downstairs happened to be locked, she would be certain to catch me.

I felt a rippling sensation down by back, down my legs. She was right behind me now. But I did not run, and I did not look back.

Something whipped past my eyes, fastened around my throat. Briefly I smelled paint and turpentine. Then I was aware of nothing except my tortured hunger for air. Hands clawing at the paint-soaked rag, she had tightened around my throat, I turned and twisted wildly, trying to break free. There was a roaring in my ears, and a red mist gathering before my eyes. My lungs felt on fire. In another moment, I was sure, the very bones of my neck would snap.

How was it that my air-starved brain finally told me what to do? I don't know. I only know that I stopped trying to break free of that agonizing pressure around my throat. Instead, fingers flexed, I managed to turn around far enough to rake my nails down her face.

Her hands dropped from that noose, flew up to protect her face. I was free. Dimly aware that the paint-stained rag had fallen away from my throat, I headed toward the doorway.

I was out in the hall before she caught me again. Grasping my shoulder, she spun me around. Blood streamed down her right cheek. Her eyes blazed, quite literally blazed. Arms flailing, I fought off the hands that sought my throat.

Somehow I again broke free. I ran. But after a split second I realized that I had not headed for the descending staircase and possible escape from the house. Instead I was running toward stairs that led upward.

No help for it. No turning back, not with her right behind me with her long arms, her maniac's strength. Dimly aware of the burning pain in my throat, I fled up the stairs, turned at the landing. A long hall stretched ahead.

Halfway down it a door stood open. As I ran toward it, expecting every instant to feel her hand grasping my shoulders or tightening around my bruised throat, I saw part of a washbasin through that open door.

A bathroom. Bathrooms had locks.

I swerved, darted inside the room, whirled around, slammed the door. I turned the thumb latch. Then I leaned against the panels, utterly spent.

Her fists pounded against the door. "Open up!"

And then she went away. I could hear her retreating footsteps. I still leaned against the door, dizzy with relief, but wondering if and when she would be back.

After a moment or two I looked around me. Walls painted a shiny yellow. Plain white fixtures. Skimpy towels on the rack above the tub. Plastic curtains at the narrow window. Obviously a servant's bath.

The servants. Even if I managed to emit something resembling a scream—and my aching throat told me that I could not—Consuelo would never hear me. Johnny Whitecloud might, but even if he summoned up enough courage to come up here and investigate he would never side with me against Rachel Gainsworth.

I moved to the narrow window. No chance of escape that way. No trees nearby, no vines on the stone walls. Just a sheer drop to that flagstoned terrace three stories below.

Perhaps Lawrence Gainsworth would return soon. Or perhaps by now that sly and vicious fragment of her shattered personality, that fragment that called itself Joe, had subsided into dormancy.

Something hard struck the door. I whirled around. She must have crept down the hall on stockinged feet, or perhaps wearing those paint-stained moccasins, because I had not heard her approach. The door shook under the impact of another blow. A panel split with a shrieking sound. And then I saw it, the sharp stone edge of a tomahawk.

I did scream then. Only a thin, strangled sound came out. The axe's stone edge withdrew, struck another panel.

Then, through the sound of rending wood, I heard footsteps pounding on the stairs, and someone calling my name.

The running footsteps were out in the third-floor hall now. I heard him shout, "Rachel! Stop that!"

Something heavy clattered against the floor. I heard the panting sounds of struggle.

Relief washed over me, bringing with it a dizziness, a sense of darkness closing in. I felt myself crumpling to the floor.

Even before I opened my eyes I was aware of the cold tile beneath my outstretched body. But there was something soft under my head. I realized it must be a pillow brought from one of the bedrooms.

I opened my eyes and looked up into Ben Farrel's anxious face. He gave me a tense smile and asked, "Better?"

I wanted to answer, but only a croak came out. He said, "Don't try to talk." Gently he touched my throat. "Does it hurt a lot? Just nod or shake your head."

I nodded.

He said, "In case it's not clear in your mind, Rachel Gainsworth went crazy. I think she meant to kill you."

For the first time I became aware that the bathroom door, no longer held by its upper hinge, leaned against the wall at an odd angle. Evidently he'd broken it in.

I whispered, "Where—"

"Where is she now? I had to handcuff her to the stair railing."

I asked, still in that whisper, "Did Dot Canby—"

"Tell me you'd come up here? Yes."

"But why did you—"

"A guy who worked at the post office phoned me. He'd been off sick when that letter was delivered to you. That's why he hadn't called me about it sooner. But anyway, he remembered seeing Gainsworth's chauffeur drop a blue envelope into the box in front of the post office last Tuesday."

I understood then. Once Ben knew that the letter perhaps had come from this house, he realized I might be in serious trouble.

"Now just lie there quietly," Ben said. "I'll phone over to Bolton for an ambulance."

Footsteps in the hall below. Lawrence Gainsworth's voice calling his daughter's name.

Ben left me. A moment later I heard him call from the head of the third-floor stairs. "Up here, Mr. Gainsworth."

Laboriously, one hand grasping the old-fashioned tub's rolled edge, I got to my feet. I stood for a moment, swaying, and then moved to the doorway. Hand grasping the door frame, I looked toward the head of the stairs.

Rachel, one hand cuffed to the stair rail, dark head drooping, sat on the floor with her legs curled around her. I could tell it was Rachel. Not Joe, who had strangled a little girl. Not bubbly Althea, who loved to paint. Not Dorothy, who did still lifes, and whom I may or may not have met. But poor, shy, chronically depressed Rachel.

Her father stood there, hand on the newel post. From the agony in his face I knew that he had already summed it up: Ben's presence, and his handcuffed daughter, and the stone axe on the hall floor, and me standing, with a bruised and swollen throat, beside the shattered door.

Ben said gently, "I'm sorry, Mr. Gainsworth, but I'm afraid your daughter was trying to kill Miss Channing. Do you have any idea why?"

Lawrence Gainsworth's voice, like his face, was filled with pain, "Yes, I think I know why. It's all my fault. But you see, when I invited Deborah to this house that night, I thought Rachel was—all right. She had been for almost five years."

I knew he did not mean "all right." Poor Rachel had not been that since early childhood. He meant only that the fragment of her shattered personality that called itself

Joe had been quiescent for a number of years.

Who or what had caused Joe to emerge? Stomach knotting up, I realized that probably it was I. An awareness that I was out here, searching for Daisy's murderer, had caused the monster to stir and then spring forth.

Gainsworth sank down on the top step and began to stroke Rachel's bowed head. "Please, Ben." His voice broke. "Just let me take my little girl to the sanitarium. Then I'll turn myself in to the authorities in Bolton and tell them everything."

CHAPTER
TWENTY-ONE

WATERY MIRAGES GLEAMED on the asphalt highway as the persimmon-colored Mustang sped north toward the prison. I looked at Ben sitting beside me, one hand on the wheel, face expressionless, dark glasses shielding his eyes from the bright afternoon sunlight.

All over, I thought.

Not just because, in the last five days, I had learned the rest of Daisy's and Rachel's and Lawrence Gainsworth's story, although I had. And not just because my father would go free now.

No, it was all over because the next day I would be taking the plane to New York and in all probability would never see New Mexico or Ben Farrel again. I had to leave.

After all, I had to work for a living. And anyway I couldn't spend the rest of my life in a little town like Prosperity.

Especially not when the guy hadn't asked me to.

I said, "How long do you think it will be before my father is released?"

"About a week should do it."

In a week he would be able to leave that gray place forever and join me in New York.

"Do the bruises on my throat show?" I didn't want my father to actually see them, even though the report given him by the county prosecutor's office in Bolton must have included the information about Rachel's attack on me.

"No," Ben said, glancing at me, "not with that turtleneck sweater."

A nurse had bought the sweater for me, a light blue one, a few hours before I left the hospital in Bolton.

It was in the hospital, too, that I learned what Lawrence Gainsworth had done that day twenty years in the past. Sitting beside my bed, Ben had given me the details of Gainsworth's sworn testimony before the county prosecutor.

After Lawrence Gainsworth had knocked

Rachel away from her victim, and locked her up in the smaller studio, he had stared down in panic at the strangled child.

"He realized he should have gone to the police," Ben said to me that day in the hospital. "But I can understand why he didn't. He knew that it would not undo Daisy McCabe's death. What would happen would be that his only child would be imprisoned for life in a hospital for the criminally insane. And so he decided that he must hide Daisy's body where, if and when it was discovered, it would never be connected with the Gainsworth house."

But with one broken arm and a broken collarbone, how could he accomplish that? How could he manage to place Daisy in either his Jeep or his flatbed truck, drive well out into the desert, dig a grave in the hard earth, and then replace the dirt and smooth it over? He simply could not. And of course, he did not dare to turn for help to the chauffeur in his employ at that time, an elderly Norwegian.

And then the answer came to him. Johnny Whitecloud would dispose of the small body. True, Johnny could not drive a car. But he could ride a horse.

Lying there in that hospital, I had

thought of how painful that decision must have been for Lawrence Gainsworth. He had raised the retarded Indian from early childhood. He must have looked upon him almost as a son. But of course his own flesh and blood was even dearer to him. What was more, if Johnny was caught, society would not do much to him, a man with the intelligence of a seven-year-old.

Nor did Gainsworth have to fear, as he would have with anyone else, that Johnny Whitecloud, if somehow apprehended before he disposed of the body, would reveal how it came about that he was carrying a strangled child. If Gainsworth told him to remain silent under any circumstances, then he was almost certain to do so. Toward Gainsworth the Indian had the unswerving devotion of a dog to its master.

And even if Gainsworth had felt that there was a chance that the Indian might betray him, he still would have enlisted Johnny's help because there seemed to be no other way out of his dilemma.

He placed Daisy's small body behind a stack of blank canvases in one corner of the studio. He released his daughter—his weeping, bewildered daughter, who had no idea of why she had been locked up—from the smaller studio and, with soothing words walked with her to her room.

That night, after he was sure that Rachel and the servants were asleep, he carried a blanket to the studio. Despite the fact that he had the use of only one arm, he managed to wrap the small body in the blanket. (No, he told the county prosecutor, he had not been aware that anything was clenched in her stiffened fingers. Both fists were clenched. He had thought it was the result of a death spasm.) He carried her down the back stairs and out to the stable, which in those days had stood among the pines. He left Daisy there, went to the room above the garage where Johnny slept. He awoke the Indian and told him to accompany him back to the stable.

Johnny had been used to wandering over the hills and desert as freely as a wild animal at all hours of the day and night. Still, he must have been frightened indeed when he learned what was expected of him. But he obeyed wordlessly. He helped Gainsworth tie the blanket-wrapped bundle, along with a short-handled shovel, behind the saddle of a bay mare.

Gainsworth made Johnny repeat his

instructions three times. He was to bury the body someplace in the desert a long way away, at least several miles beyond the other side of Prosperity. And he was to be sure to bring the blanket and shovel back with him.

I pictured the young Indian—in his twenties then—riding over the desert that night, circling well north of the sleeping town, and continuing east. I wondered just when it was that he recalled that Joe Hartley and his wife and little girl, who had gone away someplace, had left a hole already dug in their backyard. Just by digging it wider and deeper, he could rid himself quickly of his frightening burden.

I thought of him there in that barren yard, shoveling the hole three or four feet deeper. Remembering that first he must remove the blanket, he placed her in her improvised grave and covered her over with earth. After that, I imagine, he might have wrapped the shovel in the blanket and tied it on behind the saddle. Certainly he must have gotten away from there as soon as he could.

Gainsworth had spent the night—an overcast one, with now and then a distant mutter of thunder—in the stable. He had been waiting, not only for Johnny Whitecloud's return, but for the start of the heavy rain the ten o'clock news had predicted. If any aspect of this tragic affair could be considered lucky, a rainfall heavy enough to obliterate the mare's hoofprints would be lucky for Gainsworth.

Johnny returned about an hour before dawn, a few minutes after the first large raindrops struck the stable roof. Relieved by the rain's onslaught and by the fact that Johnny had remembered to bring back both the shovel and the blanket, Gainsworth did not question the Indian's statement that he had placed the body "in a hole, a long way away." In fact, Gainsworth did not want to know exactly where the child's body lay. If he could, he wanted to put behind him the previous dozen hours.

I could imagine what a paralyzing shock it must have been to him to learn that the child had been unearthed from Joe Hart-ley's backyard. Hartley, a man whom Gainsworth, like almost everyone else in town, both liked and respected.

His guilt must have been tremendous, although not so great as to make him reveal that his daughter had strangled Daisy. He had tried to assuage his guilt in other ways, providing my mother with enough money to take herself and me to New York, striking up a correspondence with my father, and sending him books to make prison life less grim.

Lying there in my hospital bed, I wondered why it had not struck me as odd that Gainsworth, fond as he appeared to be of my father, made no mention of visiting him. Writing to a man to whom you have done such a grievous wrong is one thing. Facing him is quite another.

That afternoon in the hospital I said to Ben, "I suppose it was Gainsworth who shot at me as I was coming back from the arroyo."

"Yes. That night you had dinner at his house he had learned that you were absolutely convinced that someone else had killed Daisy McCabe. He was afraid that even at this late date someone as strongly motivated as you were might manage to get some inkling of the truth. When Gainsworth's scared he doesn't think too clearly. That's why he had the bad judgment to try to frighten you away with a few rifle shots."

I knew what Ben meant by bad judgment. Those shots had only deepened my conviction that it was someone else who belonged in that prison.

I said, "Where is he?"

"Gainsworth? At his house, I suppose, if he's not at Rachel's sanitarium. He posted bail, of course."

"What will happen to him?"

"Not much, I imagine. After all, he was trying to protect his daughter. A jury might sympathize with that."

I had left the hospital the next morning. Ben's deputies had retrieved my rented Datsun from the driveway of the Gainsworth house by that time. I found it waiting for me in the hospital parking lot.

Aware that the prison officials had already been notified of Gainsworth's confession, I called the warden's office as soon as I got back to my hotel room. The warden himself came on the line. Yes, my father had been given a copy of Lawrence Gainsworth's statement. Yes, he knew he would be released unconditionally. And certainly I could see him the next day at any time I chose.

"And not in the visiting room, Miss Channing. Your father is no longer in the cell block, but in a room in the gardener's quarters." The warmth in his voice told me

268

how pleased he was to be able to say that. "I'll see to it that you can meet him in one of our vacant offices here."

A few hours later I phoned my boss in New York. He was out, but I gave his secretary the message that 1 would be back to work the following Monday. She asked if anything was wrong with my throat. Without the desire or the voice power to talk about it just then, I said, "Laryngitis."

I had just hung up when Ben telephoned. "I suppose you'll be going up to the prison soon."

"Tomorrow."

"We might as well drive there in my car, I've got some business up at the prison. A fellow my father arrested for check forgery two years ago is coming up for parole, and the warden wants to talk to me about him."

"All right."

"Pick you up about one?"

"Fine."

And so now we were driving across desert flats and through low, juniper-studded hills toward the prison, he apparently deep in his thoughts and I deep in mine.

So for me it was back to New York and

the singles scene. But now it wouldn't be the rich girl's singles scene, bounded on the east by the Hamptons and the west by Bloomingdale's, with outlying suburbs in Gstaad and Marrakech. Oh, maybe I would keep a few of my former friends, at least for a while. But perhaps the wire services already had carried the full story of how one Joseph Hartley had served twenty years in a New Mexico prison for a crime he didn't commit. Much as they might sympathize with both him and me, the very fact that my father had spent all those years of enforced association with men convicted of violent crimes would make them feel uneasy around me. Unjust, of course, but that was human nature.

Well, what was I kicking about? I had a good job. When the duplex and the East Hampton house were sold, I would have a few thousand in the bank, which was more than a lot of people had. Best of all, I would have my father with me, and might be able to make up to him somewhat for all those lost years.

So why was I kvetching?

Well, I wished Ben Farrel would stop acting as if the New York plane, with me aboard it, had already taken off.

The gray walls loomed up ahead. Ben showed identification to the guards at the gate, and we were waved into the parking lot.

CHAPTER
TWENTY-TWO

INSIDE THE PRISON we parted. Ben took the elevator up to the warden's office. I followed a guard down a ground-floor hall to a small office, empty except for a desk and two straight chairs and a filing cabinet. The guard told me he would send my father to me right away. Then he went out, closing the door behind him.

A few minutes later the door opened and my father walked in. He wore brown trousers and a brown V-shaped sweater over a white shirt and a brown-and-white striped tie. The brown shoes they had provided for him looked cheap, but they had a beautiful polish.

We smiled at each other. Suddenly I felt very shy, and I could tell that he did, too.

Then I cried, "Oh, Papa! You look so *nice.*"

I went into his arms then and we both wept. After a while I stepped back and wiped away my tears and blew my nose. He said, "Are you all right, honey? I know you had a bad, bad time."

"I'm fine, Papa."

"You're sure?"

"Of course I'm sure."

He said, after a moment, "I don't suppose you've seen Lawrence Gainsworth."

"Not—not since that day. I understand he's out on bail."

"I hope they go easy on him." Then he laughed. "Don't look at me like that, Debby. I'm not bucking for sainthood. It's just that he must have been in his own kind of hell this past twenty years with me on his conscience all the time.

"Besides," he added, "I don't—want to be bitter. I want to enjoy the rest of my life."

"I'll help you enjoy it, Papa."

"I know you will."

"When can you leave here?"

"The warden thinks that by next Wednesday all the red tape should be unwound."

"I have to fly to New York tomorrow. But you come there as soon as you're released. Phone me first, so I can meet you at Kennedy."

Suddenly he looked embarrassed. "Deborah, I'm not going to New York."

"Not going?"

"I knew you'd ask me, honey, so I've thought the whole thing through. I don't belong back there. I belong in the town where I grew up. I've got good friends there. Jay Barnwell, for instance."

"The man who owns the service station?"

"That's right. He's been in touch with me. He and his wife want me to come to work there. I'd like that. Maybe I'll put money into the place, if he and Bee want new equipment. I'll have some money, you know. Maybe quite a lot. The warden says that the state will pay me compensation.

"Now don't look like that, honey. We'll see each other often. You'll fly out here to visit me. I'll visit you in New York, and we'll paint the town red. Now let's sit down, honey. I want to hear about your job. Your mother wrote in one of her letters that you were thinking of trying to be a statistical analyst, but she didn't say what that was."

I was still explaining about statistical analysts when the same guard who had led me here poked his head around the edge of the door and smiled at us. "Excuse me, folks, but the warden wants to see you, Hartley. Needs you to sign some papers." He withdrew his head and closed the door.

My father and I kissed good-bye, and I cried a little more while he patted my shoulder, and then he left. After lingering a few minutes to repair the tear damage, I walked out of the prison.

I found Ben Farrel behind the wheel of the Mustang. I asked, "Have you been waiting long?"

"Five minutes, maybe."

Neither of us spoke again until we were out on the highway. Then Ben asked, "How's your father?"

"Fine. Just wonderful. But he doesn't want to come to New York. He wants to live in Prosperity. Would you have believed it?"

"Sure. After twenty years in an eight-by-ten cell, New York would be just too much for him. Besides, he has friends in Prosperity."

"So he pointed out."

We drove in silence for perhaps five minutes. Then he said, "I suppose you'll be marrying that guy now."

I said, astonished, "You mean Greg? Whatever gave you that idea?"

"Well, it figures. Your father's not a con anymore. He'll be a free man, with an official apology from the state and compensation money to boot. So why shouldn't you and that guy get together again?"

"Because the situation hasn't been altered enough, not for people like Greg's family. To them I'll still seem—tainted, somehow, not acceptable. As I told you, I don't blame them. When they welcomed me as Greg's fiancée, they had no idea that my father was in prison."

"But what about this Greg himself? You may be okay in his book now. What if he decides to go against his family?"

I thought for several moments. Then I said slowly, "If he did, he might regret it later on. And anyway, I believe I've changed so much that I don't think I'd want him now, even if he said he wanted me."

With a sense of wonder, I realized that was quite true. I wasn't the same carefree, somewhat pampered girl who, sitting with friends on the terrace of that beach club, had seen the handsomest man she had ever known walk toward her.

Still, it was going to be a tough business, living alone in New York, and hoping that one of those "better fish in the sea" my father had mentioned would swim my way—and that I would fancy him if and when he did.

We drove another mile or so in silence. Then Ben said, "In that case, maybe you wouldn't mind if I looked you up."

I turned and stared at him. He continued to look straight ahead. His face was still expressionless, but I could read tension in the way his hand gripped the wheel.

I said, "What do you mean, look me up?"

"In New York. You see, a couple of nights ago Dad told me he's decided to retire. Said he feels it will be more fun hunting bobcats than check kiters and coke smugglers. At first I thought maybe he just wanted me to feel free to leave Prosperity, but after I talked to him for a while I saw he was on the level. And so, with him not needing me to back him in his job, I thought I'd go to New York and finish up my courses at the Police Academy."

Quite suddenly, as I looked at that carefully expressionless profile and that betrayingly tense hand, I knew what people meant by the phrase, "my heart swelled." It's an exhilarating, lighter-than-air feeling.

The idea of going back to New York didn't bother me now, not one little bit.

"Why, no," I said. "I wouldn't mind if you looked me up."

The publishers hope that this Large Print Book has brought you pleasurable reading. Each title is designed to make the text as easy to see as possible. G. K. Hall Large Print Books are available from your library and your local bookstore. Or you can receive information on upcoming and current Large Print Books and order directly from the publisher. Just send your name and address to:

G. K. Hall & Co.
70 Lincoln Street
Boston, Mass. 02111

or call, toll-free:

1-800-343-2806

A note on the text
Large print edition designed by
Bernadette Montalvo
Composed in 18 pt English Times
on an EditWriter 7700 by
Genevieve Connell of G. K. Hall Publishing Co.